A vacation in Mo~~n~~
"Bones" Bonebrake i~~n~~
adventure centering a~~round a monumental discovery.~~
The remains of giants, mammoth beings from antiquity,
are laid out before him. Most appear to be long since
decayed, but one does not.

Looking like it—she—only recently died, the
enormous woman's perfectly preserved corpse is a find
like no other, a real-life "Queen of Giants." And when
the excavation team suddenly disappears overnight,
Bones quickly realizes that there's more to the
mysterious find than meets the eye.

PRAISE FOR DAVID WOOD AND THE DANE MADDOCK ADVENTURES!

A great read that provides lots of action, and
thoughtful insight as well, into strange realms that are
sometimes best left unexplored." Paul Kemprecos,
author of Cool Blue Tomb

"Dane and Bones.... Together they're unstoppable.
Rip-roaring action from start to finish. Wit and humor
throughout. Just one question - how soon until the next
one? Because I can't wait." Graham Brown, author of
Shadows of the Midnight Sun

"David Wood has done it again. Quest takes you on an
expedition that leads down a trail of adventure and
thrills!" David L. Golemon, Author of the Event Group
series

SKIN and BONES
A Bones Bonebrake Adventure

DAVID WOOD
MATT JAMES

Skin and Bones
Copyright 2018 by David Wood
All rights reserved

Published by Adrenaline Press
www.adrenaline.press

Adrenaline Press is an imprint of Gryphonwood Press
www.gryphonwoodpress.com

This is a work of fiction. All characters are products of
the authors' imaginations or are used fictitiously.

ISBN: 978-1-940095-96-7

BOOKS and SERIES by David Wood

Arcanum
Magus (forthcoming)
Brainwash
Herald (forthcoming)
Maug (forthcoming)
Cavern

Jade Ihara Adventures (with Sean Ellis)
Oracle
Changeling
Exile

Bones Bonebrake Adventures
Primitive
The Book of Bones
Skin and Bones (forthcoming)
Venom (forthcoming)

Jake Crowley Adventures (with Alan Baxter)
Blood Codex
Anubis Key

Brock Stone Adventures
Arena of Souls
Track of the Beast (forthcoming)

Myrmidon Files (with Sean Ellis)
Destiny
Mystic

Sam Aston Investigations (with Alan Baxter)
Primordial
Overlord

BOOKS and SERIES by MATT JAMES

The Hank Boyd Adventures
Blood and Sand
Mayan Darkness
Babel Found
Elixir of Life

The Hank Boyd Origins
The Cursed Pharaoh (coming soon)

The Logan Reed Thrillers
Plague
Evolve

Standalone Novels
Dead Moon

Co-Authored Projects
With David Wood
Berserk
Skin and Bones
Venom

Prologue

The morning mist covered the rolling hills in a blanket of gray. Andron shivered, but it was not the chill in the air that elicited the reaction. It was something deeper, more primal. Something very wrong.

"I do not like this place one bit." He gripped the hilt of his sword, but found scant comfort there.

"And I do not like your constant complaining. At least we are alive." Phidias stood, arms folded, staring into the swirling cloud ahead. "Would you have preferred we drowned like the others?"

Andron didn't reply. Their ship had been caught up in a storm and quickly capsized. As far as they knew, only he and Phidias had made it to shore. Clinging to broken bits of their ship, they'd managed to drift ashore during the night. Now, exhausted but desperate, they were heading inland in search of fresh water.

"Where do you think we are?" Phidias asked.

Andron shook his head. They'd been blown off course, and then drifted for hours. There was no telling where they were. All he knew for certain is they were a long way from Greece.

"We should move to higher ground. Once this fog burns off, perhaps we can get some idea of what our next move should be." Phidias didn't wait, but turned and marched up the hill. Heaving a weary sigh, Andron followed along behind them.

They marched along in silence, the soft ground cushioning their footfalls. Andron kept slipping on the slick grass, each time falling a little farther behind. His cheeks burned every time Phidias shook his head or chuckled. Andron was the youngest member of the crew—when there had been a crew—and Phidias took full advantage of his higher status, ordering the younger man around every chance he got, and mocking him at every turn.

If it turns out we're stranded on a deserted island, I'm going to cut his head off first chance I get.

"Stop!" Phidias halted, drew his sword. "There's something up ahead."

Perhaps Andron should have been concerned, but instead he was relieved to have an excuse to draw his weapon without drawing his companion's scorn. He slid his sword free of its scabbard and gripped it tightly.

They began to move forward again, one cautious step after another. A light breeze stirred the fog, and out of the mist a dark figure suddenly loomed. It appeared human at first glance, but it couldn't be! It was impossibly large, tall and broad of shoulder.

"What is it?" Andron whispered.

"I…" Phidias moved his lips but could not form words. He took a step back, then another, his olive skin turning pale. "M… monster?" he managed. "Cyclops? Giant?" He took another step backward, slipped, and fell on his backside.

Up ahead, the figure inched closer.

Or did it?

And then Andron realized what they were looking it. Relief flooded through him and he barked a laugh.

"It's a statue. The swirling mist gave it the illusion of movement."

"Oh." His face now scarlet, Phidias clambered to his feet and stalked toward the statue. Andron followed along, grinning.

Up close, their mistake seemed laughable. At least, he found humor in it. Phidias was busy trying to forget his embarrassment from moments before. The figure had an overly-large forehead and a thin, wedge-like nose. Deep eye sockets cast shadows on spiral-carved eyes, symbols of magic. They were impressive, but wholly alien in appearance.

"I wonder who carved him?" he said.

"There are more." Phidias pointed up the hill. The sun was peeking over the horizon and the fog thinning to reveal more of the imposing figures arrayed on the hillside.

"It's like they're standing guard," Andron said.

Phidias frowned, and tugged at his thick, black beard as he gazed up the hill. "But guarding what?"

"I suppose we'll find out if we keep climbing."

They resumed their trek, winding through the forest of statues. All were sculpted to represent fighters: soldiers armed with swords and round shields, archers, even gloved boxers. And all stood a good three heads or more taller than the two men.

"What if these are the actual size of the men who carved them?" Andron asked.

"Nonsense." Phidias had reverted to his brusque manner. "They carved them larger than life to make them more impressive or intimidating."

"A few minutes ago you believed in giants and cyclopes."

Phidias ignored him.

Up ahead, a flash of motion caught Andron's eye. Something large was moving among the statues.

Something huge!

"Phidias! We need to go right now! Back down the hill!"

Phidias ignored him and quickened his pace, making a beeline for the place where something lurked.

Andron saw it again—a shadowy figure every bit as tall and broad of shoulder as the statues that gazed sightlessly into the distance. He froze.

"There's something up there!"

Phidias looked back without breaking his stride. "Joke all you want. I'll have no more of your nonsense."

It happened in an instant. Andron could only stare, rendered mute by shock and fear, as something out of a nightmare stepped out from behind a statue and swung a club at Phidias's head.

It wasn't until he heard the wet crunch of Phidias's skull shattering that Andron forced himself to run.

1

Bones Bonebrake groaned as he pried himself out of the cramped taxi. At a hair over six-feet-five-inches, even the relatively spacious rear seating area of the Mercedes sedan was a tight fit for the former Navy SEAL. As he stretched out the kinks, he breathed in the humid, salty air, and examined the façade of the building. The hotel was pristine, white, and sat right on the waterfront of Monaco. It was exactly the kind of hoity-toity place he tended to avoid—not that it would keep him from enjoying its amenities or anything. It was the people that normally stayed in such places that he didn't care for. Uptight, no fun, and all around annoying as hell.

"Bones!"

He turned in the direction of the shout and saw, emerging from the hotel entrance, the familiar face—and figure—of Yesenia Archuleta. *Jessie*, as she preferred to be called, was a radiant, raven-haired Latina. She and Bones had shared an adventure and he was eager to renew their acquaintance.

Even without the temptation of some one-on-one time with Jessie, the invitation to Monaco had been too good to pass up. All he had to do was pay for airfare. The rest of the trip, Jessie had explained, was already comped by a friend of a friend.

Behind him, the cab driver was struggling to unload Bones' sole piece of luggage from the trunk. With one final grunt, the man succeeded in heaving the large duffel bag up and over the lip of the Mercedes' hold, but as soon as it was clear, its bulk nearly threw him off balance. Bones grinned and shoved a handful of Euro notes into the man's hands.

"Keep the change, bro," he said and then effortlessly plucked the bag off the sidewalk. Noting the driver's shocked look, he added, "You have to lift with your legs."

Jessie met him halfway and practically leaped into his arms.

She wrapped her arms around his neck, stretched up to his cheek and gave it a quick peck. Her lips felt warm and she tasted of beer. Apparently, the party had started without him.

Rude, he thought, *but awesome!* Bones loved a girl who knew how to enjoy herself.

He set her down and looked her over. Jessie was wearing a skin-tight, white tank top that sported the logo of the famed Monaco Gran Prix Formula One race, one of the most prestigious motor sport events in the world, which was currently underway and was, ostensibly at least, the reason for Jessie's invitation. A temporary grandstand had been set up at the rear of the resort, facing the street which presently also served as a racetrack. The Gran Prix course was Monaco itself, the drivers obliged to negotiate a circuit that would take them through the curves and peaks and valleys of Monaco's streets.

"Hey, my eyes are up here," she remarked, but her tone was playful.

He looked up, but in his peripheral vision, saw a second girl with a matching tank come up behind Jessie. She was dark-haired and not unattractive, despite a layer of makeup so dense that it could probably deflect a high caliber bullet and a frown that looked like a permanent feature.

Bones laughed, looking back and forth between the two women, stopping on the newcomer. "Is today twin day? Not that I'm complaining."

Jessie rolled her eyes and let out a tiny laugh. "This is Rose Pacheco. She's the reason you're here."

Rose crossed her arms and thrust a hip out to the side. *Obviously, doesn't share Jessie's sense of humor.* Of course, Jessie hadn't been a big fan of his personality at first either, but Bones had eventually won her over with his indomitable charm.

"Yeah, thanks for having me," he began, "I'm…"

"I know who you are, Uriah Bonebrake." Her tone was sour, but mischief flickered in her eyes.

"That's me, but you can call me Bones."

She rolled her eyes. "You're right," she said to Jessie. "He is uptight." Nostrils flared, she spun on a heel and marched off, almost slamming into a heavyset man with a cane.

Bones looked down at Jessie. "I thought I was being friendly. What's her deal?"

Jessie giggled, a little tipsy. "Rose's boyfriend dumped her a few days ago."

"So, I'm filling her ex-boyfriend's spot? No pun intended."

Jessie nodded. "I didn't think it was important information."

He rubbed his forehead with his palm, kneading away a rising headache. "It's cool. I'll just steer clear of her if she's in a mood."

Jessie hooked an arm around his and led him forward. "We've got our own room, of course."

Bones smiled. "Now, we're talking, *Yesenia*." He exaggerated her given name and got an elbow in the ribs in return.

"Jerk."

Bones had managed to get through most of his life without forming any major attachments, but he had a soft spot for Jessie, especially after what happened to them in New Mexico. Asshats, aliens, and Albuquerque... The three A's from hell. That had been an interesting few days to say the least.

The fact that she still wanted anything to do with him afterward was a bonus. The easiest way to burn down a potential relationship was by almost getting the other person killed. And in his line of work, almost getting killed was a pretty regular occurrence.

She handed him a white, plastic card the size of a credit card.

"What's this?" he asked, looking it over.

"Besides your room key, it's also a buyer's card that's linked to your account. It'll take care of your food and whatnot while we're here."

"Wait a sec, free beer? How much?"

She grinned. "If you can consume it, it's paid for." Jessie signaled a bellhop to take care of his luggage.

Beer sounded good, and free beer sounded even better. Maybe an ice-cold Dos Equis with a lime, if they even had it on the menu in this fancy place. Or maybe a French brew like a Kronenbourg Blanch. At this point, he'd drink just about anything. His vacation had officially started and his lady friend was way too far ahead of him. But as they stepped through the front doors and into the air-conditioned building, Jessie steered him through the lobby and back outside into a courtyard that was crowded with people. Bones spied a small outdoor bar, surrounded by vacationers, many of whom appeared to be waiting to order, but Jessie steered him away, toward the pool area.

"Where are we headed?"

"The stands," Jessie replied. "We have seats next to the tightest curve on the track!"

He winked at her. "I can think of a different set of tight curves I'd rather see."

Jessie patted him on the arm and leaned in close. "Cool your engines. You just got here. Maybe if you behave yourself…" She let the words hang.

"Behave myself? Have you met me?" He lowered his voice. "So, what's the deal with your friend. Who is she exactly?" He was thinking of the unlimited credit on his room card. Somebody somewhere had serious money.

"Why does it matter?"

"Call me curious," he replied, gazing out across the pool. It was long and rectangular and had a fountain dead center in it. You could swim beneath the cascading water or even make out under it like a couple was doing now. Evidently, not everyone was in town for the race.

"She was my college roommate," Jessie explained. "For a few months anyway. Right now, she's a research assistant on an incredible dig in Sardinia. Her father is sponsoring the excavation, by the way—they're very influential people. She's not so bad, but she can act a little…entitled sometimes."

A powerful family with money and a spoiled brat for a daughter. Great…

"I'm here on summer break and volunteered to help out," Jessie continued. "The dig pays for our room and board so it's a pretty sweet deal for only a couple hours of work each day. I'll be here for two months and thought having you around at the beginning of it would be fun." She suddenly pulled away, holding him at arm's length. "You should come with us! Rose said Dr. Santi is always looking for more help, especially with Lucas not here."

Lucas? Bones thought. *Who the hell is Lucas? Oh, right, the ex.* "Uh, sure," he said grabbing her around the waist before she fell into the pool. "Sounds fun."

She rose up on her tiptoes and planted a quick kiss on his lips. He *really* liked this girl.

"You're already at it?" a disapproving voice rang out.

They parted to find Rose standing there with her arms crossed, hip out to the side like before. It seemed to be her go-to pose when her inner demon was awakened.

"There's plenty of me to go around," Bones said.

Jessie elbowed him in the gut.

"Girl, bye," Rose said.

"Just trying to lighten the mood. Sorry we got off on the wrong foot." He didn't truly believe he owed her an apology, but why not be the bigger person, figuratively as well as literally? "I do appreciate you including me on your trip."

Rose stared at him for the span of three heartbeats, as if waiting for a punch line. When none was forthcoming, she forced a crooked half-smile.

"Whatever. We need to get going if you want to see the race."

2

Bones marveled at the view spread out before him. He, Jessie, and a still-grumpy Rose—Jessie in the middle—were seated almost dead center in the stands, near the bottom of the U-shaped turn in the roadway and overlooking the incredible waterfront. Expensive-looking yachts lined the dock on the far side of the road, giving the boats' owners an up-close view of the festivities.

The first car came screaming around the corner, the driver braking and shifting as it neared the U-shaped bend. They had apparently missed the opening announcements at the race's start.

Bones smiled despite himself as the car approached and then quickly passed, accelerating out of the turn and hitting them with a sonic-boom-like concussion. As soon as the driver made the tight left-hand turn, the racecar, which looked more like a fighter-jet than an automobile, sped away and disappeared around a banking right curve, following the coastal road.

"This is so cool!" Jessie shouted, slapping Bones' thigh repeatedly.

"It really is," he agreed, impressed. Bones wasn't a racing fan, but even he had to admit that was pretty awesome.

They were near the end of the first lap, only a quarter of a mile from the finish line, and the herd of drivers had already begun to thin out. Races were normally very bunchy at the start but as the cars fell into line, they generally came by one by one. It wasn't until the last ten or so laps where the drivers started to take big chances. Once the end of the race was within sigh, they tended to drive like bat-shit-crazy high schoolers. Early on, however, they just wanted to make it deep into the contest without getting into a wreck.

"It takes impeccable reflexes and keen eyesight to succeed on this course," Rose explained, stating the obvious with authority.

Duh.

Bones shrugged indifferently. "If Tony Stark can do it, anyone can."

"Didn't he wreck after getting attacked?" Jessie asked, leaning closer to him.

"Details," he said with a dismissive wave. "He was doing just fine until Ivan showed up and cut his ride in half."

"I didn't know you were into superheroes."

He shrugged. "Just the ones that can score hot chicks."

Rose continued, not understanding the conversation about *Iron Man 2*. "Compared to your NASCAR, we Europeans have a much sleeker sport here."

"I don't like NASCAR," Bones said. "It's just hillbillies turning left for three hours."

Three more cars whizzed by, all in a row. Then, they saw the first large group. Eight cars jockeyed for position as they neared the turn, fighting one another for dibs on who got to make the hairpin first.

A red and yellow car—it was moving too fast for Bones to make out a number or team logo—went low, trying to squeeze in between a blue and white variant and the left-hand wall. The aggressor was clipped from behind as its right rear wheel was struck and lifted.

Red and Yellow went airborne, using Blue and White as a ramp. The car was launched straight into the chain-link barrier between the track and the stands, obliterating some of its body in the process. Two more cars joined the mayhem and careened into the first two involved.

That was when Bones noticed just how low and feeble the barrier on the other side of the road was. It was only around four feet in height.

Fortunately, the dock appeared to be off limits to most of the general audience—but that didn't include the people on the yachts.

A loose wheel went hurtling toward the nearest yacht. Bones gut clenched when he saw a girl—maybe six or seven years old—break from the group of panicked spectators to leap *forward* onto the dock and then hurry up and over the divider wall as the tire seemed to chase her.

She landed on the roadway and froze.

Bones was on his feet and moving before the girl hit the ground.

Trampling fellow spectators, he bounded down the bleachers, heading straight for a gap in the damaged fence. As he moved, he shouted for the astonished onlookers to "move it or lose it." Luckily, many of the spectators were already on their feet to gawk at what was happening, which gave him the opening he needed to leap the final two rows of seats. He gripped the fence, shimmied up and over to drop the ten feet to the asphalt below.

The girl was huddled against the inside wall, paralyzed with fear. Bones was about to dash across the road toward her, but before he could, two more Formula One machines rounded the bend and came barreling towards them. Both cars were fighting for control of the inside lane to avoid the problem and were evidently oblivious to what was going on right in front of them.

The second of the cars came in too hot and sideswiped Blue and White as it tried to avoid the wreck. Its rear end went sliding straight at Bones as it spun. Eyes wide, he jumped back onto the chain-link fence and lifted his lower half off the ground. He was buffeted by the wind rolling off the vehicle's spoiler as it passed beneath him.

The other car missed the girl by mere inches. The slipstream of the car's passage sucked her away from the barrier, causing her to flop forward onto the road. It was only luck that had spared her and there was no guarantee that her luck would hold. With the shape of the turn, the cars would be unable to see her until it was too late to change course.

Bones dropped down, and with only a quick glance to make sure that he had an opening, bolted across the track. Miraculously, he made it, but as he reached her, he felt the road began to tremble underfoot.

More cars were coming.

In one motion, he gripped the back of the girl's shirt and threw her over the barrier, practically falling over with her. He allowed his momentum to carry him over, tucking his legs in as he rolled across the narrow dock to plunge into the water below. The girl stayed close and he held onto her shirt before going under.

He quickly kicked to the surface all the while trying his damnedest not to let go of the girl. He wasn't sure if she knew how to swim or not and now wasn't the time to figure it out by trial and error.

They surfaced together, met with the sound of screams and sirens. A multitude of hands reached down for them. Bones helped two men hoist the much smaller girl up first, before allowing them to attempt to pull him out. It took three guys to get him back up on dry land.

He spilled to the dock and rolled onto his back and was immediately tackled by the sobbing child. A few seconds later, another man, looking a little shell-shocked, pulled her away from Bones. From the way she latched onto the newcomer, Bones guessed it was her father.

"Next time," Bones said, panting, "I won't be there to save her." He struggled to his feet. "Watch your kid."

The man frowned. Apparently not understanding English.

Bones looked up into the clear-blue, Mediterranean sky and closed his eyes. Calming a little, he opened them and looked down at the drenched girl. She appeared to be in a state of shock herself, staring off into nothing.

"Hey, kid. You okay?"

She might not have understood his words, but she got the gist. She managed a tiny smaile and a nod.

"Stay close to your old man, okay?"

Finished playing the role of lifeguard, he turned and planted a hand on the divider, easily hopping over it. His boots squished when he landed. Weaving between mangled heaps and already arrived medical units, Bones climbed back up the chain-link fence and dropped back down on the other side. The fact that he wasn't forced to dodge any incoming cars told him that the rest of the field had passed their position.

"Holy hell, Bones!"

He looked up and found Jessie standing a step higher than him, now eye level with him. He glanced down at the dribbles of water still rolling off his saturated clothes. "I guess I've got an excuse to take my clothes off."

Jessie smiled and held up her keycard. "Let's go."

3

The helicopter landed smoothly even with the strong crosswind coming off the water. When the skids kissed the small patch of tarmac, Bones let out the breath he'd been holding seemingly since taking off from Monaco. While never one to be nervous when flying, he preferred to keep his feet on the ground whenever possible. And being in a chopper brought back memories of dangerous raids in perilous situations during his days in the service. He felt like he was already pushing his luck after the previous day's incident on the race course and was ready to be out of this bird.

And being stuck in a tin can with Rose is no picnic either, he thought, climbing out of the aircraft.

Seconds later, Rose pushed past him. He quirked an eyebrow but Jessie took him by the hand before he could say anything.

"Be nice!" Jessie shouted, having to speak loudly over the din of the still spinning rotor blades. Bones nodded and helped her down. They moved off, away from the noisy machine. "You said you'd keep your cool around her," Jessie added.

"No, I didn't," he replied. "I said I wouldn't cause a scene and embarrass the uptight rich asshats."

Bones didn't remember agreeing to the Sardinia excursion when he'd accepted Jessie's invitation but he also didn't feel like hanging around the pool all day. Jessie was the reason he was here after all. She had to go, even if he didn't, and with Rose's boyfriend MIA, there was a vacancy on the roster for the archaeological dig, and an extra seat on the helicopter

Southwest of Rome, and across the Tyrrhenian Sea, Sardinia was the second-largest of the Mediterranean islands. The temperatures rarely reached in excess of 90-degrees Fahrenheit and today's high was expected to be 78. Summer wasn't yet in full swing here like it was in Florida.

I could definitely get used to this.

It was jeans and t-shirt weather and Bones loved it. Jessie was currently sporting a tight, black University of New Mexico T-shirt and a pair of hip-hugging, khaki capris, and, like always, she rocked it without trying.

They had landed outside the small town of Cabras which had the population of an ant farm—a whopping nine-thousand upright citizens. The center of town held its city hall and a church dating back to the 1600's. There was also a pretty impressive archaeological site nearby named, Tharros.

While in the air, Rose had explained that the excavation was about a half-mile away—a short walk. While they hoofed it, the locals watched intently from an uncomfortably close distance. Bones wasn't sure if it was because they'd never seen a Native American before or if they didn't trust any outsiders. He figured it was a bit of both and kept moving.

"What's their problem?" he asked when two *Children of the Corn*-types joined in. Seriously, it was bad enough when the adults gawked, but when the kids joined in, that was almost more than he could handle.

Should have brought some holy water.

"Remember the looks you got in Quemadura?" Jessie whispered.

"How could I forget?" he replied sarcastically. He'd gotten all kinds of sideways glances in that podunk New Mexico town, mainly because of some funny business going on between the sheriff, his idiot son, and a conspiratorial group called ICE. Compared to Quemadura, Cabras looked like a thriving metropolis.

"Rose told me everyone gets them here," she explained, still keeping her voice down. "Rumor has it, this place does whatever possible to avoid tourism. The mayor is a very paranoid person, apparently."

"A small Mediterranean town that *doesn't* want tourists?" Bones asked, confused.

"I know, right?" she looked around. "What a bunch of weirdos..."

You have no idea, he thought. He and Maddock had seen much, much weirder things over the years. A superstitious, or just flat out unwelcoming town wouldn't be the oddest thing he ever saw.

"Keep moving, please," Rose said from in front of them.

She glanced back and gave Bones a disapproving look.

"Eyes forward," Bones retorted. "I don't want you stealing my soul or anything."

Rose pulled ahead, huffing in anger as she did.

"I don't think your senses of humor are in alignment," Jessie said with no malice in her voice. She wasn't much different than him, really. Plenty of attitude to spare, which was probably why they got along so well.

"She'll warm up to me."

Jessie laughed. "No, she won't. She surrounds herself with abrasive guys. Loves the drama."

Bones stopped and mimicked Rose's angry

posture, hands on hips. "Whatever," he said, tossing his head and slinging his long black hair.

His smile faded as more and more people began to gather around them. They stood just close enough to make things uncomfortable. Bones rarely felt self-conscious, but something triggered his self-defense instincts. His right hand reflexively balled up into a fist.

"Relax, killer," Jessie said, noticing his growing discomfort. She took hold of his fist and forced his fingers open, sliding hers against his palm. "Just go with it. The site is clear of everyone not a part of the crew. The only people that'll give you a problem are the people you step on."

"Is that size discrimination, shorty?"

Jessie rolled her eyes. Then she smiled wide. "Believe me, you aren't the biggest person here."

He looked around and did the math. Everyone in Cabras was at least six inches shorter than him. "You sure about that?"

She smiled. "I never said they were alive..."

"Huh?"

"The dig," Jessie said. "It has something to do with the Mont'e Prama giants."

The name brought up a recollection—something he'd read or seen in a History documentary. Then, it came to him. "Stone sculptures don't count."

Found by accident in the early seventies, the Mont'e Prama giants were thirty-some-odd stone statues, between six and eight feet in height, discovered in caves not far from Cabras. The statues had been attributed to the little known Nuragic civilization that had inhabited Sardinia before the rise of Classical Greece.

Jessie laughed. "Rose told me that they are some of the oldest anthropomorphic sculptures in the Mediterranean region—minus Egypt, of course."

"But that is not why we are here," Rose said, over her shoulder.

"We're just trying to have a conversation, chick."

Rose stopped and faced them, her expression stern. "When you see what Dr. Santi has uncovered, you will apologize for your rudeness."

"If you say so."

"You will see," Rose said, with a cryptic smile before turning and resuming the trek.

"What's she talking about?" he asked Jessie in a hushed tone.

"I...I don't know." Her eyes met his. "This is news to me. They've kept the findings here to themselves, only saying that it was related to the original Mont'e Prama site."

Crap, he thought. When secrets were kept, and history made, things seldom turned out well. People always associated a historical find with fame and fortune, hoping to get rich quick, but it rarely worked out that way. Something usually went horribly wrong.

"Damn you, Dr. Jones," he mumbled to himself.

"What?" Jessie asked, half hearing him.

He shook his head. "Nothing. Just stay close and keep a watch for anyone, or anything, suspicious."

The problem with that advice was that every one of the locals gawking at them seemed suspicious.

The site sat just east of Cabras Pond, a serene, partially man-made lagoon. Three large flatbed trucks were parked between the hole and the coast. One of them was outfitted with an industrial-sized jib crane.

There was a church nearby, one of several he'd seen during the walk, and a cemetery with old, weathered gravestones. The close proximity of the latter only added to the uncomfortable feeling digging its way into Bones' spine.

Jessie elbowed him, and gave him a start. "You still with me?" she asked, worried.

"Yeah, I'm good," he replied, blinking hard. "Just wish we were somewhere else a little less foreboding."

"Come on," she said, laughing. "It's not that bad."

"Recent heavy rains caused a section of the coastal road, *Via Messina*, to collapse," Rose explained. "Witnesses said that the water pooled here instead of draining out to sea like it was supposed to. The weight of the water caused the already fracturing road to give way. When the water eventually drained away, it revealed a hidden cave system."

Bones gazed down into the sinkhole. The pit itself was about forty feet across and a good thirty feet deep. It had been cleared of all debris to reveal a mostly flat floor, and in the center, a large sarcophagus. A small team of workers, presumably Dr. Santi's research crew, moved around it, which helped Bones estimate the length of the sarcophagus.

"Easily over ten feet tall." He saw Jessie nodding in his periphery. He looked at her. "Is there a body in there? A… a giant?"

"Rose says they're opening the lid tomorrow." She patted his arm. "Maybe you'll get to use those muscles for something other than punching people."

"I haven't hit anyone yet."

She grinned. "Yet…"

He rolled his eyes and checked out the

surrounding area, cataloging everything he saw for later. It was a habit drilled into him during his years as a SEAL; you never knew when things would go south and knowing the lay of the land might mean the difference between life and death.

"Where's this Santi dude?"

Jessie pointed down into the hole. "Right there."

Santi was a small man, not just shorter than everyone else working in the pit, but slightly built as well. He looked like he might blow away in a stiff breeze. From the higher angle, Bones couldn't get a look at the man's face beneath his baseball cap.

"Yesenia!"

Bones looked in the direction of the voice and found Rose waving from across the excavation. She motioned for them to come over and join her. Reluctantly, Bones followed Jessie and they made their way around to the other side. As he did, Bones was given a different perspective of the layout below. At this angle, he could see a tunnel to the east, heading deeper underground, in the direction of the town.

Interesting...

They passed behind the trucks and eventually found Rose standing at the top of a ladder bolted directly to the stone wall.

"Come, this is what I wanted to show you," Rose said as she swung out onto the top rung and began her descent. "I did not dare mention this while out in public. I could not risk anyone overhearing."

Jessie glanced at Bones and shrugged, then she too swung out onto the ladder and began climbing down. Bones waited for Rose to finish and for Jessie to get halfway down before adding his weight to the ladder.

Unsure of who attached the ladder, he wasn't about to trust just anyone. He didn't see anyone who he'd describe as "qualified" labor nearby. For all he knew, Rose installed it herself. The last thing he needed was to fall thirty feet and break his legs or back.

Maybe even both.

When his feet hit solid ground again a shout echoed from inside the eastern tunnel and he spun to find a young, college-aged woman running out of it. She tripped and slid across the stone flooring, taking out two more people with her. Bones helped her up but recoiled in alarm when he saw the expression on her face.

It was a look of sheer terror.

4

Bones thrust the frightened woman into Jessie's arms, and took off down the tunnel, grabbing a shovel as he went. He didn't know what had spooked the woman, but if it was alive, it was about to get a spade across its head. He just hoped that would do the trick. He was otherwise unarmed.

Ten feet in, he came to a light. It was mounted on a stand and pointing down so people didn't trip over its base. There was another light ten feet further along, and then another. After the fourth such light, Bones saw that he had reached the end of the passage. He slid to a halt, gripping the long handle of his shovel.

He was in a circular chamber, almost like the one behind him. The biggest difference was that this one was perfectly preserved. Statues of giants—vaguely human figures with smooth features that looked uncannily like C-3P0 from the Star Wars movies—encompassed the space, surrounding the center of the room like a family of watchdogs. Three other passages, each pointing in a cardinal direction, were visible in the low light.

North, south, and further east.

Six lights were situated along the outer wall, one in front of each statue. A seventh light at the center illuminated what lay there.

"No way…"

It was another sarcophagus, just like the one in the other chamber, except this one was open, the lid resting off to the side. But that wasn't the only difference.

"Holy crap," he said aloud, peering down at the cadaver nestled inside. "It's real."

"She, actually."

Bone whirled about, shovel raised like a club. Luckily for the man who had startled him, Bones didn't swing. Nevertheless, the diminutive figure let out a yelp of alarm and sprang back.

"Dr. Santi?" Bones asked.

"What is wrong with you?" he shouted in thickly-accented English. He had wisps of his thinning hair dangling over his eyes as he spoke. "You could have killed me!"

"Sorry about that," Bones said, "but you nearly gave me a heart attack. One of your people came running out of here, hollering like a Howler monkey, so I came in ready to swing."

Santi huffed but composed himself as Rose and Jessie arrived.

"Yes, well only a few of us have seen *her* so far."

Rose went straight for Santi and Jessie headed for Bones. She only made it halfway. When she saw the corpse, she ground to a halt.

Like the archaeologist said, it—*she*—was most definitely a female. Her curves were obviously those belonging to a woman. Even hidden beneath the mummy-like wrappings, that much was obvious.

Bones patted Santi on the shoulder and stepped towards the body. She was easily ten feet tall but was proportionately built. Her bone length and muscle girth was as if Jessie increased in size without losing anything anywhere.

"Who is she?" Bones asked, looking back to Santi.

"We do not know," he replied, combing his hair back with his hand and replacing his hat. "There are symbols on the pedestal, but they're unlike any language I've ever seen."

Bones knelt and inspected the writing. He didn't recognize a lick of it.

"What happened to the lid?"

Santi crossed his arms in frustration. "Who exactly are you?"

Bones stood. "Someone with a lot of experience with this kind of stuff."

Santi didn't respond.

"You can trust him, Doctor," Jessie said. "Believe me, he's seen a thing or two."

"And why should I trust you so easily, Ms. Archuleta? I've only just recently met you as well."

Rose stepped forward. "Because I can vouch for her." She looked at Bones. "Him, I don't know about, but he's got a reputation for knowing about…unusual archaeological finds," she said begrudgingly.

The archaeologist looked uncomfortable but answered. "We think that the queen was only just recently buried."

"Queen?" Jessie asked.

"Recently?" Bones asked.

Santi looked at Jessie. "It is what we are calling her." Then to Bones. "The corpse is extremely well preserved. There's hardly any decomposition. If I didn't know better, I'd almost think she was laid to rest only a few weeks ago."

"No freaking way," Bones said, looking at the body.

He leaned in close and looked at the shape of her

face, following it down to her shoulders and chest. The wrappings were opaque but thin, and clung tightly to the corpse like a second skin, leaving very little to the imagination.

"That's a whole lot of woman."

"Yes, she is," Santi agreed.

Bones' eyes flicked to Jessie and he waggled his eyebrows. She frowned and shot a meaningful glance in Rose's direction. Her meaning was clear.

Rose just vouched for you. Now is not the time to act like an assclown.

"The wrappings appear Egyptian," Jessie said, moving in for a closer look at the dead woman.

Santi shrugged. "It's not entirely unheard of for the practices and traditions of one major civilization to spread to other regions and be absorbed by other cultures."

"It's only a hop, skip, and a boat ride across the Mediterranean from Egypt to here," Bones added, earning a nod from Santi. "You can see the influence of Egypt all around the world."

"The Washington Monument," Jessie said, "Paris and the Vatican too."

"Bingo," Bones said, giving her a smile. "And Vegas."

Santi gazed up at Bones and managed a smile. He held out his hand. "Dr. Valentino Santi, mister..."

Bones shook the hand, careful not to crush it. "Bones Bonebrake, but everyone just calls me, Bones."

"His real name is Uriah," Rose quickly added, knowing exactly how to get under his skin.

Santi must've seen his reaction to hearing his birth name and didn't repeat it. "So, Mr. Bones, what exactly is your field of expertise?"

"Marine archaeology is my trade, but I've been on my share of digs.Let's just say I've got a knack for finding unusual things. Some of them valuable."

"A treasure hunter?" Santi looked skeptical.

Bones nodded. No point in lying. "Among other things, yes. But I take my work seriously. I'm not a tomb raider." That wasn't always true, but this wasn't a time for splitting hairs. He clapped Santi on the back. "But I'm on your side, Doc. I didn't come here to steal your thunder."

"Why are you here then?" Santi asked, turning to him. Bones wondered if he grilled all his volunteers like this and decided to be upfront with him.

"She invited me." He nodded at Jessie, who blushed.

Surprisingly, Santi smiled. "Oh, I see."

"Dr. Santi," a voice called from down the tunnel. "The mayor wishes to speak with you."

The archaeologist removed his hat and brushed back his thinning hair. "Just wonderful." He glanced up again at Bones. "Mayor Leonardo Giolito. He likes to check up on us. He is disappointed that he cannot get any more involved, so instead he makes a nuisance of himself."

"Why's that?" Bones asked.

"We labeled this as an offshoot of the original *Giants of Mont'e Prama* discovery and took control of it for conservation purposes." He pointed to the encompassing statues. "See their faces—the circular carvings on their cheeks?"

He looked and, for the first time, saw them. "What's so special about those?"

Santi shrugged. "No one knows, but the Prama sculptures have them too. We named this 'Site B.' The mayor was none too pleased with it."

"Why would it matter?" Jessie asked.

"I was hoping that the findings here would tell me," Santi said, "but, so far, we've come up with nothing. I think the people in town know something, something in their traditions, but no one will answer any of my questions—very uncooperative people around here."

"I kind of got that impression from the sideways glances we got coming in," Bones said. "They don't like outsiders."

"You think this site is the reason?" Jessie asked.

Santi just scratched his chin, squinting at Bones. The project leader was called for again and he cursed under his breath and headed for the tunnel. "We shall continue this conversation over drinks tonight. Signorina Pacheco, you will arrange everything, *si*?"

Rose nodded at the man but looked annoyed.

"Later, bro."

Santi stopped. "Bro?"

Bones waved him off. "Whatever, dude, I'm not drawing a check or nothing. We'll just see you later." Without a word, Rose left with Santi, heading back the way they'd come.

Bones turned to Jessie. She looked worried.

"If someone in Cabras knows the real story about this place," Jessie said. "They might be willing to cause trouble to keep it from getting out. We'll need to be extra careful."

He nodded, thinking the same thing. "Whenever there's a sacred tomb, hidden from all mankind, there's always some whackjob who'll stop at nothing to keep it that way." He recalled the people staring at them as they walked through town. "Maybe more than one whackjob."

Maybe an entire townful...

5

That evening, they met at a local *trattoria*. They were given a table at the center of the main room, perfect for everyone there to watch them. Bones wasn't an idiot, he knew what the hostess was doing. As they sat, Santi had mentioned that the owner was also the sister of the mayor.

Just another entitled family, Bones thought, sitting so he faced the door in order to keep a watch on the main entrance.

Jessie sat to Bones' left and Santi to his right, which left Rose in the chair opposite him, across the square table. She glared at him as if her eyes could burn a hole right through him.

"To our discovery." Santi raised his glass in celebration.

They all repeated the toast and clinked their glasses together.

"Tell me something, Doc," Bones said, catching Santi's eye while the other man drank, "what's the deal with everyone here—and don't tell me it's because we're outsiders. Plenty of tourists visit Sardinia all the time." Bones leaned forward on his elbows, speaking as low as he could. "What's *really* going on here?"

Even Rose looked interested in hearing what Santi had to say.

"There is a story around these parts, and the eldest of families believe in it wholeheartedly."

Bones grinned. "Legend, folklore, mythology…

Whaddaya got?"

Santi thought for a second. "A bit of them all actually."

"I'm guessing it has something to do with our queen?" Bones asked.

"It does, yes," he replied. "The giants of myth were said to be of demon blood, if you believe in that sort of thing. The most famous of them were the Biblical Nephilim, born of fallen angels and human women."

Bones kept his expression blank. He knew firsthand that those stories were not entirely mythological. "You think the queen was a creature from the Bible?" he asked.

"Hard to know anything at all, but some believe that she may have been part of a lesser known species. While not *evil* in the context of good versus evil, she belonged to a wretched race of cannibals and warmongers."

"They have a name?" Bones asked.

Santi appeared to hesitate before answering. "There's little known about them at all. The only reason you ever heard about it is if you were born here or knew who to ask."

"How do you know then?"

Santi looked at him. "I was born in Cabras, Mr. Bones. I only lived here until I was seven, but I heard all the tales when I was a child and thought them to be only ghost stories. It was not until the tomb was discovered that I begged my superiors in Rome to let me lead the excavation here. Happily, they thought my intimate knowledge of the area was a good fit and sent me."

He took a sip of his wine. "There are stories about the queen, too. Some believe that she was the last of her race, hidden away and cared for underground by a select few. They worshiped her as a goddess and tried multiple times to find her a mate."

"A mate?" Jessie ask, looking a little green.

"Yes. And any mate would do," Santi replied. "At least, they were willing to give anyone a try."

For the next few minutes, they just sat and enjoyed each other's company. Bones finished his drink and motioned to the waitress for another while Jessie and Santi talked about the incredible weather and then about the local cuisine. The mention of food made Bones' stomach growl.

The only one that didn't partake in the conversation was Rose.

Bones glanced over at Rose. "You're awfully quiet."

She met his stare. "I have nothing to say."

"Really?" Bones asked, acting shocked.

"Really," she replied, with a smirk.

"See," Bones smiled at Jessie, "I'm growing on her."

He grinned and turned back to the archaeologist. "Anything else about the site that would hold value to this place beside the loony toons who worshiped the hell spawn below?"

Santi thought for a moment but held his tongue as the waitress dropped off another round of drinks. The local woman lingered for an uncomfortable few moments before finally turning and leaving.

He spoke again, keeping his next words hushed. "There may or may not be undiscovered wealth within the necropolis."

"What kind of wealth are we talking about?"

Bones asked, trying not to act too interested.

"The original Mont'e Prama find has a necropolis that still has not been excavated. You saw the tunnels down there. If this is a part of the same culture, why not build one here too? There could be an entire city of the dead down there waiting to be explored."

"How far have you in have you gone?"

"That's what she said," Jessie mouthed, forcing Bones to cover his guffaw with a cough.

"Not far—just to the queen. Patience is very important with a discovery of this magnitude."

Before Bones could enquire further, he saw three men—thick-set, barrel-chested locals, stand up and begin heading toward them. In an instant they were positioned in a triangle around the table. One stood over Bones' right shoulder and another over his left.

Crap. Can't a guy get a normal vacation with a hot chick and 'not' have to fight for his life?

Bones felt someone nudge his foot under the table and watched as Jessie pounded the rest of her drink. She then spun the heavy glass mug so the handle was pointing his way.

Smart girl.

He held up a finger, signaling the men to hold on a minute, while he also downed the rest of his drink. He had actually planned on nursing it, not draining it like he would've in his younger days. Santi must've understood what was about to happen and he likewise finished his. Bones rolled his eyes when he saw Rose cross her arms and sit back. She'd be no help at all. She confirmed as much when she nonchalantly pulled out her phone and began typing.

The third man, the one behind Rose, started

circling the table like a hawk, looking very confident in himself and his friends.

"Can we help you?" Santi asked politely.

"Yes, you can." His English was clipped, but easy enough to understand.

"How?" Jessie asked, her hand fidgeting under the table. Bones could feel her leg bouncing, rubbing against his own.

"By leaving," Number Three replied. "We do not want your kind here."

"But it's such a nice town," Bones said, setting his glass down. "I hear the nightlife around here is to die for. I think I saw something on *E! News* last week about a Kardashian renting a summer home up the coast."

The guys behind Bones made their move but he was ready. He punched the one on the right—Number Two—in the groin just as Jessie stamped down on Number One's foot. It stalled his attack long enough for Bones to spring to his feet and punch the man square in the jaw, sending him to his knees.

He grabbed Jessie's empty mug and smashed it onto the back of Number Two's head. The handle broke off in his hand as the glass shattered into pieces. The guy went down, startling Santi. Bones quickly drove his knee into the side of Number One's head before he could get up. The man crumpled to the ground beside Jessie's chair, unmoving but alive.

Number Two staggered as he got to his feet and swung an out-of-control fist at Bones. Using the dazed man's momentum to his advantage, Bones hip-tossed the man onto the table, which collapsed under the sudden addition of his weight. Jessie, Rose, and Santi leaped away from the broken mess in front of them.

Bones turned his attention to Number Three. The guy didn't move an inch, standing as still as the statues in the dig.

"This is how it's going to work," Bones said, calmly retying his pony-tail. "You're going to drag your buddies out of here—after paying for the damage to the place. If you don't—"

"What happens?" Number Three asked putting on a show of defiance. It looked like he was used to getting a good deal of respect from the locals, but Bones wasn't a local, and he wasn't impressed

He pointed to the front window. "You leave the hard way." He held up the broken handle from to Jessie's beer mug. "And you'll take this with you, and I don't mean you'll be holding onto it."

The man reflexively took a step back, covered his own backside with his hands.

"Nico!"

Number Three turned to the sound of the voice. The woman who had seated them, stomped over, got right into "Nico's" face and let fly with a torrent of angry Italian.

Bones laughed. "I guess you'll be paying for the damage after all."

"What is going on here?"

Bones swung his attention to the entrance and saw a small, fat man with rosy cheeks and a horrid combover, standing with hands on hips, looking in disapproval at the destruction and the two unconscious men laying in the center of the room.

"Mayor Giolito!" Santi said, "Your brother-in-law attacked us." He nodded at the woman. "Vivianna should be thankful it did not get any worse."

"Lies!" Nico shouted, pointing a thick finger at the archaeologist.

"Sorry," Rose said, holding up her phone, "but it is true. I streamed whole thing on *Facebook Live*. I can replay it for you if you like." She turned to the mayor. "Your family is now plastered all over the internet acting like swine."

Giolito's face reddened.

Bones fixed Rose with an appraising look. "Holy crap, girl! I guess I was wrong about you."

They took their dinners to go and headed for the inn where they were assigned private rooms, a special treatment considering that most of the other crew members, graduate students included, were either bunking together or camping out near the dig site. It was one of the only places nearby that would accept them as patrons. Santi knew the owner, apparently.

The three of them entered the inn together. The bed and breakfast-style place was three stories tall and had no elevator.

The archaeologist had stayed behind to iron things out with the mayor and make sure they weren't charged with criminal mischief. Bones knew that small towns like this could get away with a lot if they wanted but Rose's quick thinking had more or less saved their asses.

"Good thinking back there," he said to Rose, as they made their way up the staircase.

"Really?" Rose replied. "A compliment from you, of all people?"

Bones scratched his chin, trying not to take the

bait. He took a deep breath. "Seriously. They probably planned that confrontation back there to make us look like trouble-makers."

"A setup?" Jessie asked.

Bones nodded.

"It is not like anyone jumped in to help us either," Rose added. "Everyone there was content with us getting beaten senseless."

"Well, we didn't exactly get our asses kicked," Bones quickly said.

Rose shook her head. "You can't protect all of us all the time."

"You might be surprised at what he's capable of," Jessie said before Bones could respond. "Just stick with us and you'll be fine."

Bones' shoulders sagged. He had been hoping for some alone time with Jessie. "Does this mean she's bunking with us tonight?" he asked quietly.

"I think it might be a good idea," Jessie replied. "Just in case."

Damn it. He nodded, knowing she was right. "Fine."

Rose laughed without humor. "Forget it. There is no way I'm wearing my nightie in front of you. Besides…" She dug into her purse and pulled out a handgun, "I can take care of myself."

"Holy crap!" Bones smiled. "Screw her warming up to me; I think I'm warming up to her. Can I get a look at that?"

She flipped it around and handed it to Bones. He gave it a once-over and finished with a nod of approval. It was a Glock 26, a smaller variant of the pistol he favored. He eased back the slide to make sure there was a round chambered, then handed it back to her. "Don't take this the wrong way, but you do know how to use it, right?"

"Like I said. I can take care of myself."

The inn only had two floors of bedrooms. The ground floor housed the kitchen, storage, and the lobby. Bones and Jessie's room was in the front corner of the top floor and Rose's was next door. Santi's was on the first floor, just around the corner from the stairwell.

Bones and Jessie stopped in front of their room as Rose continued to hers, waving goodnight. Jessie opened their door and entered but Bones didn't immediately follow her, waiting to make sure Rose made it inside her room. He knew he was being overprotective, and maybe a little paranoid, but the people of Cabras were giving him the willies.

Something was definitely amiss here.

Their room wasn't anything special, just one large space. A king-sized bed took up most of the left-hand section while a small kitchenette, couch, and TV filled the other half. The only other room was the bathroom and the shower was barely big enough for one person let alone two. He was honestly surprised that the room even had its own shower. Bones had spent the night in plenty of places that sported shared commodes and baths.

Jessie had quickly changed into an oversized t-shirt and apparently nothing else, and slipped under the covers. Bones was about to join her but decided against it. He was still on edge and not comfortable with getting comfortable. Jessie's cell phone rang, disrupting the quiet inside the room. When she answered it, Bones could hear the caller's voice from across the space. *Rose.* Either the device's volume was up too high, and it made it sound like she was shouting, or something was wrong.

Jessie sat up, a look of concern on her face.

"What's up?" Bones whispered.

Jessie silently mouthed, "Santi."

Crap.

Bones kicked himself for not having insisted they wait for the archaeologist. But, like Santi said earlier, he had been born in Cabras, and he knew people here from his youth. Who would want to harm *him* of all people?

It has to be because of the dig.

Jessie ended the call and tossed the phone aside and rushed for her jeans, just as someone banged on their door. Bones looked through the peephole and saw Rose. Opening it, the Italian woman charged inside, makeup running from her eyes. She was a mess and Jessie barely got her jeans on before having to come to the woman's rescue.

Bones shut the door, locking it. "What the hell's going on?"

"Dr. Santi isn't answering his phone and the person who answered at the restaurant said he left just after we did. I called Mayor Giolito, but he said he saw Dr. Santi leave alone." Rose looked at Bones. "With everything that happened tonight, I am afraid they went after him."

Bones was thinking the same.

And why is Rose so upset? Yes, Santi is missing, and he's a decent enough guy, but she's positively distraught.

"They really are hiding something..." he murmured, getting back on point.

"What was that?" Jessie asked, fully clothed now.

Rose had gone from standing and crying, to sitting on the small couch...and crying. Apparently, she wasn't used to these kinds of things.

Like normal freaking people.

"Nothing. At least I hope it's nothing."

From the look on Jessie's face Bones could tell she didn't believe him, but she didn't press him. "I say we take a moonlit stroll by the site, maybe do a little off-the-books exploring."

"I'm in."

"Me too," Rose announced, wiping her eyes and standing.

Bones frowned. "Look, no offense, but I can't hold your hand. If things get rough, we're going to have to move fast."

Rose's face hardened. She patted her purse, where she had stashed the gun, and tried to look tough. "I'll be fine. Don't worry about me."

Bones rubbed his forehead, his frustration deepening. He was about to give her a flat out, "no" but felt a reassuring hand on his shoulder. Jessie seemed to believe in her friend; maybe she'd surprise him again.

"Fine," he said wheeling on her, "but I'm in charge and if for some reason I'm not around, Jessie is."

"You really have no faith in me?" Rose asked.

Bones quickly shook his head. "It's not about you; it's about experience. You can't really know how you'll respond under pressure until you're in the cooker." He thumbed over to Jessie. "The two of us have been through something like this before. I know for a fact she can handle herself and she won't crack."

Rose nodded, took out the pistol, and offered it to Bones. "Then maybe you'd feel better if you had this."

He waved it away. "Keep it for now. I'd rather not use one if I can help it. But stay close, just in case." Privately, he thought Rose was much less likely to get into trouble with the local authorities for possessing the weapon, given her station.

Jessie patted him on the back. "Lead the way."

Moving quickly, but without making a show of haste, they made their way down to the front entrance. Before they did, they tried Santi's room on the second floor. After knocking three times, all with no answer, they left.

The inn was just around the corner from the *trattoria* and a quarter mile from the site. The night breeze coming off the lagoon was cool and comforting.

As they passed the restaurant, Bones nodded to Rose. "Pop in and double-check to see if Giolito's story checks out."

She nodded and slipped inside.

A few seconds later, Rose came out and shook her head. "Nothing new."

"So," Jessie said, "the dig?"

"Looks like it," Bones replied. They crossed the street and continued down the road toward the archaeological site, keeping to the shadows when possible. It was after ten o'clock and most of the nightlife seemed to be toward the center of town. The coast was pretty much clear of anyone.

"Dr. Santi had a few of the grad students keep watch overnight," Rose explained. "They were to be accompanied by two guards as well."

"How many?" Bones asked, slowing as they approached.

"How many what?" Rose asked from behind.

"People at the site, how many?"

He glanced back at her and saw her head nod in the moonlight. "Oh, eight total."

They skirted the cave-in again and continued past the ladder to the crypt below. It was quiet, which wasn't good. There were supposed to be eight people here. From what Bones could tell, there were none.

Motioning for Jessie and Rose to wait, Bones hustled over to the trucks and checked each one. He was hoping that the students had gotten sleepy and passed out inside the cabs. But one after the other, he found them empty. Not even the guards were there.

"Not a single person," Bones said. He waved the girls over. "Look around. Someone must've left behind some sort of clue."

As he said this, he spotted something on the ground between the tents and the ladder.

"That's not good," he said, kneeling beside the object—a ball cap, identical to the one Santi had been wearing earlier.

Could be his.

And it was soaked in dark crimson.

"Oh, God…" Rose gasped.

Bones looked over at her, worried that she was going to lose it, but she straightened and nodded. She was trying to keep it together, and so far, was mostly succeeding.

We'll see how long 'that' lasts, Bones thought. The bloody hat was a pretty good indicator that there would be a bloody head somewhere in the vicinity.

He tossed the hat aside and went straight for the ladder, staying low. From above, he could barely make out the sarcophagus below. With a nod to the two women, he began descending, moving slowly to avoid making any noise. Halfway down it occurred to him that he should have asked Rose for her Glock, but he wasn't going to turn back now. Instead, he continued to the bottom and silently dismounted the ladder, avoiding the still illuminated lights when he could. As soon as he was down, he ducked low behind the large sarcophagus, using it as cover from the tunnel to the east. If there was any funny business going on down here, that's where he guessed it would be since it was in the direction of the queen's corpse.

And I bet the mayor's family knows all about this, he thought. *Probably why they've been trying to get rid of us.* Giolito, his sister, and her husband, Nico... They wanted the outsiders gone.

Regardless of the family's motivation to keep the find under wraps, it still didn't reveal the 'why' in all this. Why keep it a secret at all?

"Ugh," Jessie said as she stepped up next to Bones.

He was looking around the side of the sarcophagus and had to look up to see what had prompted Jessie's reaction. When he did, he noticed she wasn't looking at him, but rather behind him, at the enormous burial chest, just inches from his head.

He groaned. He'd missed it when he first approached, more worried about the tunnel and anyone that could be coming out to meet them, but now he saw it clearly.

The stone lid was spattered with blood.

6

Rose started to scream, but Jessie quickly covered her friend's mouth with her hand. The only sounds that came out were a muffled sob and a series of muted snorts. After a few seconds, she nodded, signaling that she had regained her composure, and Jessie let go.

"Should we call the police?" Rose asked, sniffing back a fresh set of tears.

Bones locked eyes with Jessie but shook his head. "No, that won't do us any good if this is what I think it is." He elaborated. "Small towns like this have their own little secrets and conspiracies, and if the mayor's involved, there's no telling who we can trust."

"What do we do?" she asked, wiping her cheeks.

Bones stood. "We figure out what the hell is going on before there's any more blood spilled." He looked at Rose. "In the morning, we can call somebody higher up the food chain and tell them what we found, but as of right now, the only evidence we have is some blood. That's not enough to get their attention."

"It could even be blood from an animal," Jessie said. "Maybe the people responsible are into ritualistic sacrifices or something. Dr. Santi said he was born here. He could be involved and hiding the truth from us."

"Like a cult?" Bones asked. He hadn't thought of it.

"Valentino is no cultist!" Rose hissed.

Bones and Jessie looked at the flustered woman, then each other.

Hmmm... First time she's called him something else besides Dr. Santi.

Jessie shrugged, her eyes lingering on Rose for just a moment before answering Bones. "Uh, yeah... A cult." She glanced at Rose again. "It is just a theory..."

"We aren't accusing Santi of anything," Bones quickly added, reassuring her. "Like Jessie said, it's just a theory."

Rose blew out a long breath, looking more in control of herself. "And what would this hypothetical cult worship?"

"Maybe them," Jessie said, knocking on the stone lid.

Bones looked up into the night sky and breathed in the fresh air one more time. Then, he stepped around the sarcophagus. The passage would lead them past the burial chamber of "the queen" and continue into a system of passages beneath Cabras—Santi said as much. He knew from experience that the tunnels could extend throughout the entire island too.

Not seeing any light within the passage ahead, Bones pulled out a small Maglite and placed a red filter over the lens. It wouldn't be as easy to spot from a distance, and the tint would help preserve his already sharp night vision.

They quietly moved down the passage, to the second chamber. Bones stepped out between two of the six massive statues and immediately noticed something different.

"What the... Where'd she go?"

"What?" Jessie asked. She had to step around Bones' larger frame to see what he did. She gazed at the *empty* pedestal and froze.

Rose was next to see it. "Please do not tell me she got up and walked away."

"Oh, God," Jessie croaked, "I hope not."

Bones held his hand out to Rose. "I'll take that gun now."

She handed it over to him. "Maybe we should just head back to town."

"Don't worry," Jessie promised, smiling at her friend. "As long as we're with Bones, we're safe."

Bones wished that Jessie hadn't said that. They were anything but safe right now. The giant woman's vanishing act was just another layer on the horror-story cake.

A soft but chilly breeze suddenly blew in from behind them, and Bones heard both women shuffle forward.

"Anyone else's sphincter pucker up just now?" Bones asked, keeping his voice down.

Only Jessie answered with a soft, "Yep."

Rose however seemed to have lost the ability to form words, which was fine by him. The last thing Bones needed was for her to squeal and reveal their presence. He shook his head, wishing he'd grabbed her gun up in the room and locked her in the bathroom. When they had just been looking for Santi, she was merely an impediment, but with the added potential for a violent encounter, she was becoming a serious liability.

"Why are you really here?" he asked her. "And don't say it's for college credits or for some on-the-job training. It's pretty obvious you have zero interest in the dig."

Her eyes found something else to look at besides him. Her embarrassment confirmed something Bones had been suspecting ever since she burst into their room, bawling her eyes out. "You're hooking up with him, aren't you?"

Jessie snorted and covered her mouth. She came around and tried to act serious, half-growling, half-laughing. "Bones!"

But this time, Bones wasn't joking. He folded his arms and kept staring at Rose. Her unwillingness to refute the outrageous accusation was as clear as any confession.

"Well?" Jessie asked, wanting an answer, and when she didn't receive one she could only stare at her friend in disbelief "That's why Lucas dumped you, isn't it? He found out about the affair so he went back to Rome, leaving you to be with a man twice your age."

"You mean to tell me," Bones said, "that you cheated on your boyfriend with a guy who's old enough to be your father, hell, maybe your grandfather, and who also happens to be your boss on a dig sponsored by your actual father?" He shook his head. He wasn't surprised, but it was gross.

"We are in love." Rose said, still avoiding their stares.

"Holy crap." He looked at Jessie. "You never can tell with some people, can you? I guess now we know why she was so eager to come looking for him." He shook his head. "Speaking of which, we should keep moving."

He headed into the passage, with Jessie close behind him. They didn't wait for Rose, but after a few seconds, she followed along.

At the far end, they emerged into a chamber like the first two, but without statues or branching tunnels.

There was one other major difference; a body lying atop the closed sarcophagus—a regular human-sized body. The smell of death was heavy in the air.

Gun up, he checked the domed room but found it empty, save for the body.

"You may want to stay back here," he said, and then started forward. Jessie took a breath and followed, which didn't surprise Bones, but Rose stayed put.

The body was that of a young man, though it was difficult to be sure of even that. His head was caved in, his facial features misshapen, and the flesh of his extremities and torso had been ravaged, stripped to the bone in some places. Bones couldn't tell if he was one of the missing students or one of the guards. He shone his light on the dead man's thigh where several distinctive round wounds confirmed his worst suspicions.

Jessie swallowed before speaking. "Cannibals."

Bones agreed. The bite marks were definitely from human teeth, not an animal.

"Didn't Santi say the giants here were cannibalistic?"

Jessie nodded in the dim, red light. Then, her eyes met his. "You think maybe we're dealing with a cult of worshipers that mimic their...god?"

Bones recalled the matching corridors surrounding them. "If all these passages lead to other chambers like this, they're might be more bodies in each."

The prospect of a mass feeding made him sick to his stomach, but when he led the two women back to the central chamber and took a different passage, his fears were at least partly allayed. Instead of another burial chamber, the long, gently descending tunnel opened up and brought them to a tall an iron gate—a relatively new one, judging by the lack of corrosion. Bones estimated the barrier to be around ten-feet-tall. It was also the first indication that the site had been visited in the modern age prior to Santi's explorations.

There were glistening spots of wetness on some of the bars. Whoever or whatever had devoured the guy in the other burial chamber had evidently passed through the gate afterward.

Bones handed his flashlight to Jessie. Gripping onto a dry part of the gate, he gave it a push. The gate was heavy but swung inward without a sound.

"Let's go," he said, taking back his light. Leading with the pistol, he started forward, heading deeper into the unknown.

7

After another fifty feet, the tunnel transformed into something that looked more like a den than a tomb. Short passages to the north and south led to secondary rooms. In one, they saw crude tables and benches.

"A dining room?" Jessie asked, swallowing hard.

Bones was thinking the same and gave her a grim nod in reply. He hoped they *weren't* used for that but if their suspicions were true—if someone had decided to continue an ancient culture's obscene tradition of sacrificing and consuming human flesh, then they were definitely dealing with some sick people.

"They aren't covered in blood," he finally said. "The guy back there was slaughtered—fresh. These look clean and well kept. Maybe we've got the wrong idea."

He glanced at Rose and was surprised to see her handling the situation better than he expected.

"The site is on the main road heading east," she observed, her voice quiet but calm. "If we continue along this path, we will go directly under the center of town."

"And what's there?" Jessie asked.

"Well, among other things, city hall."

Bones frowned but was hardly surprised. "Giolito."

"Fabulous." Jessie said. "This hellhole just happens to pass beneath the center of a town controlled by a man that does whatever he can to avoid outside eyes." She looked up to Bones. "What are the odds they aren't connected?"

He shook his head. "Zilch."

"Do you really think Mayor Giolito is behind this?" Rose asked softly.

"We don't exactly have an airtight case," Bones replied, "but he's my prime suspect." He played his red light into another room but didn't see anything different than the last few. "Why do you care if he is or isn't anyway?"

"He and my father go way back—Dr. Santi too."

Bones stopped and turned. "Explain."

Rose glanced at Jessie, but the other woman didn't flinch. She also wanted to know.

"They were business partners for a number of years but Giolito eventually left the financial world for politics. My father met Dr. Santi through the mayor a number of years later."

"If he was such a big shot, why become mayor of this podunk town?" Bones asked.

"Like Dr. Santi, Mayor Giolito was born here. He said he wanted to return to his roots."

Bones took a deep breath. Things were beginning to make sense... Sort of. Something had happened to bring Giolito back to Cabras.

"I think the mayor, or people he trusts, found something down here and they want to keep it hidden." He glanced at Rose. "Your father being friends with Giolito and also Santi's benefactor might just be a coincidence, but me and coincidences don't exactly see eye-to-eye."

She stomped to a halt. "My father...!" Bones put a finger to his mouth. She quieted. "My father has nothing to do with this besides sponsoring the excavation."

Jessie put a gentle, apologetic hand on Rose's shoulder before falling into line behind Bones. He could just make out an arched opening up ahead. They were about to emerge into another chamber. The fact that the tunnel was getting brighter with every step taken, filled him with both hope and dread.

Here we go.

Nearing the opening, Bones saw that the illumination was actually firelight. They'd be able to see what the next chamber held without the need of his Maglite. Clicking it off, he peeked out into the gaping space, groaning at what he saw.

The warmer air makes sense....

The chamber was large and fairly deep. The floor sunk away beneath them, accessible by a crude and large stepped, stone staircase at each of the four cardinal points. They knelt at the western entrance and took in the sight.

"These steps weren't made for people," Jessie said, kneeling next to him.

He nodded in agreement.

In the center of the room sat an enormous throne—far too large to accommodate an ordinary human—covered in sheets of what looked like gold. The surrounding area was lit by a ring of small fires which burned in the spaces between the four staircases. In front of each fire was an altar, at least, that's what they reminded Bones of. Like the throne, they also appeared to be made of gold, but the shimmering metal was streaked with a dark brown substance.

Bones was pretty sure it wasn't rust.

The chamber appeared to have been carved out of a natural cave, into something resembling a bowl, with the throne at the bottom. The roof still sat untouched by the people responsible for constructing such elaborateness. Stalactites hung low in some places, giving the foreboding throne room an even creepier feel.

"Are those skeletons?"

He had been so transfixed on the glint of gold and the overall scope of the room, that he had not taken the time to examine the ground itself. Now he saw it clearly. Thousands of bones littered the floor in the space between the fires and the stairs. He couldn't estimate the age of the remains from where he was standing. Some may've been centuries old, while others may've been more recent than that.

He stood and took a step down the oversized stairs, feeling Jessie's hand latch onto his. He looked over his shoulder and eyed Rose who shook her head and stepped back into the shadows of the tunnel.

"Okay, just stay put," he said, and continued down the steep decline with Jessie in tow.

"Looks like they worshiped the queen, just as Santi said," Bones whispered.

"But who?"

"No idea, Giolito maybe?" He glanced back at her. "You still with me?"

"I'm scared shitless, but I'm still here, aren't I?"

He gave her a reassuring grin and finished the descent, stepping out into the bone-filled clearing. The only parts of the amphitheater-like chamber that weren't covered with the dead were the central walkways. They formed a circle around the throne, connecting with each of the four staircases. Someone was maintaining the room, keeping the fires lit.

To his left and right were golden altars—and

that's what they were. Both were stained dark brown too.

Bones turned his attention to the king-sized throne and gazed slack-jawed at its construction. It was low-backed and wide at the base. Nothing fancy but still incredible. Even at six-five, Bones would have felt puny sitting upon it—not that he wanted to.

A chorus of voices spooked them both and sent Bones into motion. He grabbed Jessie by the wrist and pulled her behind the closest altar, to the northwest of the throne. After a few seconds, with the voices getting louder, he risked a peek around the corner, and saw a column of hooded figures come marching out of the eastern tunnel to begin descending the stairs toward the throne.

He ducked back and glanced over at Jessie.

She mouthed. "What do we do?"

"Stay put until we're asked to leave," he whispered, and then held up Rose's gun to remind them both that they were not entirely helpless. "Remind me to go over the finer details of our next get-together a little better."

She gave a sheepish shrug.

He concentrated on the voices. He didn't recognize the language but immediately noted that they seemed to be chanting the same phrase over and over again, no doubt part of a ritual prayer.

He poked his head out again and watched as the six cloaked newcomers encircled the throne, still chanting in the unknown language.

Then, one by one, they drew back their hoods and revealed themselves.

He instantly recognized, Mayor Giolito—no surprise there. Ditto for the second and third cultists—

Vivianna, Giolito's sister, and her husband, Nico. The next two were Nico's buddies from the bar fight. Now that he saw them together again, Bones noticed a family resemblance. Brothers maybe.

But the last person's identity stunned Bones. Jessie squeezed his arm hard, barely holding back a gasp of disbelief. Number Six slowly removed his hood, exposing the diminutive Dr. Valentino Santi.

Bones mentally kicked himself for not figuring it out sooner. The man they were trying to find was involved in this mess the whole time. Santi leading the excavation was the perfect ruse, too. The cave-in had already exposed the network of tombs to the world so there was nothing they could do about that. But as the man in charge, he'd be able to keep an eye on everything while posing as only an interested archaeologist with local ties. If a discovery *was* made, he'd be able to sweep it under the rug before it got out.

Santi would report that nothing else useful was found, and Giolito would continue to make everyone visiting the town uncomfortable. Whatever he was telling the local populace about outsiders was subterfuge to keep this place a secret. They'd be able to close it off to the public and go about their lives, business as usual.

Suddenly, a shriek tore through the hum of the chant. Rose. "Valentino!" she screamed. "How could you?"

Crap, Bones thought. *So much for staying put.*

8

Rose's scream drew the attention of the six cultists. Three of them—Nico and the other two men from the bar—started up the steps toward her. They didn't appear to be armed, and Bones wasn't going to shoot the men in cold blood, but he knew he had to do something.

He thrust the little Glock into Jessie's hands. "Cover me."

Then, he planted a firm hand atop the golden altar and drove down with his legs, vaulting up and over it in one smooth motion. As he came down, he lashed out with his right foot, catching the closest cult member—Mayor Giolito—in the side of the head. The man went down like a ton of bricks.

Rose was still screaming, albeit less coherently, but Bones ignored her and pounced on the next closest cultist—Santi. He charged the slight man and bulled into him from the side, knocking him off his feet, sending him sprawling into one of the bone piles. Vivianna promptly retaliated by leaping onto Bones' back and pounding at him with her fists, but he swiftly pried her loose and flipped her toward the throne. She slammed into it with a thud and cried out in pain, holding her hip.

Bones balled his fist to meet her next attack but was caught from behind by Santi. Shrugging out of the older man's grip, Bones wheeled on him and drove a knee into his gut. Stumbling back, the archaeologist tripped over Giolito and fell backward into the same altar Bones had just vaulted over. His head hit with a *thud* and his body slumped to the side, definitely down but not completely out.

Jessie popped up, brandishing the gun, but didn't seem to know whom to aim it at. Bones pointed up the stairs to where Nico and the others were turning to join the melee. She swiveled toward them and shouted, "Stop!"

The trio froze, realizing that she was serious.

Bones blew out his breath and turned his attention back to the others. Vivianna was conscious but clearly in pain, crawling toward her dazed brother. Giolito was still unconscious but breathing.

Santi roused, startled awake from Jessie's shouted order. The gun went to him next since he was now the closest of the threats.

"Please, Mr. Bones," he begged a groggily. "Let me explain."

The plea surprised Bones, but Santi didn't really look like someone who had just chowed down on a feast of human flesh. Had he gotten this wrong? "All right," Bones replied. "Explain."

"No, Valentino," Vivianna protested through clenched teeth, "you must not tell—"

"They need to know if they are going to help."

"Help?" Jessie laughed. "You expect us to help you monsters?"

"Jessie's right. We found one of your human sacrifices. Eaten." Just saying it turned Bones' stomach.

Santi climbed to his feet, using the altar for assistance. "We are not monsters. But they do exist. Or rather, *he* does."

Bones ground his teeth together, frustrated by the cryptic explanation. "He who?"

Santi nodded at the throne.

Bones groaned. "Let me guess. There's a king, too?"

The other man nodded. "And he is not in a particularly good mood since his beloved was killed in the cave-in. I was trying to keep the excavation centered on the single chamber but my team showed up a day early and moved into the second chamber without my knowledge. Her body wasn't meant to be found."

"Is that why Giolito it?" Jessie asked, putting together the pieces.

"We were hoping to report the disappearance as a theft. You two were going to be blamed."

"Then, the mayor would have been be able to officially take over the site and close down the excavation." Bones said.

"Where it would stay closed forever," Santi confirmed. "The secret must be preserved. He must not be threatened any more than he already feels."

"He," Bones repeated. "And you guys worship him. Provide sacrificial victims for late night snacks."

"We worship him to appease him and spare the town above. We are all that stands between him and disaster. But you are wrong. We do not provide human victims." Santi's lips twitched into something like a smile. "Despite what you have seen, his tastes are not that discriminating. He'll eat any kind of meat as long as it's fresh."

"Where is he now?"

The man's face dropped. "On his way here. We were summoning him with our prayers."

Bones' heart sank. "Crap." He turned to Jessie who quickly shoved the gun into his hand. "Time to go."

Bones and Jessie started for the stairs, but the loud thump of fast moving, oversized footfalls from the eastern passage told them they were already too late.

The king stepped through the eastern tunnel, loudly sniffing the air as he did. He was completely hairless and deathly pale, no doubt the result of centuries of living underground. Lean, with muscles rippling under nearly translucent skin, he looked human enough, aside from his towering twelve-foot height.

Bones watched as the buck-naked giant ducked through the ten-foot-tall archway to enter the room. As soon as he was inside, his eyes instantly locked on the two intruders. Circular grooves were carved into the flesh of his cheeks, right below his eyes. The patterns were the same as on the statues surrounding the queen's pedestal.

So far, he and Jessie were spared, but after Rose let loose another scream, it got the king moving. He squatted, opened his arms out wide, and roared. Mid-bellow, he began his descent.

Leveling his gun at the giant, Bones unloaded three quick shots. Each struck the king dead center in the chest but the only effect was to piss him off.

"Move!" he shouted.

Giolito rolled out of the way as did Vivianna, dragging the still senseless Giolito, but instead of fleeing, they huddled together near the base of the throne. Nico and the other men, already standing on the steps, turned and fled.

Jessie needed no further encouragement. She turned and bounded up the steps, pumping her arms furiously as she ran. Bones managed to keep up, taking the enlarged steps two at a time, but as he neared the top, he felt the floor shake beneath him. The tremor caused him to stumble, and he cracked his knee painfully on one of the stone steps. He grunted in pain but took the moment to glance over his shoulder. The king was already on the lower level, passing the throne, taking enormous strides.

Bastard must've jumped!

Bones rolled onto his back and fired two more rounds—to no better effect—and then crab-walked the rest of the way up to the entrance to the west tunnel, where Jessie, Nico and the other two men were waiting.

"My wife!" Nico shouted.

Bones didn't think Giolito, Vivianna, and Santi were in any real danger; the king had blown right past them. He *hated* to leave anyone, even these three conspirators, but getting torn to pieces trying to save them was an even less appealing proposition.

"We'll figure something out," Bones promised, producing his Maglite to illuminate the path forward. He found Jessie huddled next to an almost catatonic Rose, trying desperately to pull her friend to her feet.

In one smooth motion, Bones yanked Rose up and threw her over his shoulder as he started down the passage at a dead run. Jessie and the three local men were right behind him.

When they reached the chamber with the partially consumed man, Bones heard Jessie gasp in dismay.

"What about the others?" she asked, breathlessly.

Bones was about to answer that they should probably assume the worst, but then remembered that they had someone with them who could probably confirm it. "Nico!" Bones yelled.

The local man looked up in surprise. "What?"

"Do you know what happened to the others—the ones Santi left behind to watch the site?"

Nico swallowed nervously. "He took them."

"Kinda figured that. But are they dead?" He glanced down at the carcass. "Did he eat them all?"

Nico took on a pained expression. "I don't know. They have not taken a human in decades, and only then because they were desperate. They want to be left alone and only require food every few weeks."

"Which you provide."

"We do. They stay below if we keep them fed—especially now with such easy access to the surface."

"What do you feed them?" Jessie asked.

"Livestock mostly—cows, sheep, pigs. They love beer, too."

Bones tried not to grin. "My kind of monsters." Jessie snapped her horrified gaze toward him. "I mean the beer," he added, "Not the uncooked livestock and man-flesh." He swung his gaze back to Nico. "You said they only eat every few weeks. So maybe he'd keep them alive a while. Captive stock for fresh meat."

Nico shrugged.

"Does the king have a lair of some kind?"

"About a mile east of the throne room." Nico looked like he was about to say something more, but then he clammed up.

Bones didn't press the issue. They were in no shape to attempt a rescue now. The first priority was getting back to the surface. If the rhythmic thump of giant footfalls reverberating down the length of the passage was any indication, making it out alive was by no means a foregone conclusion.

They passed the chamber with the queen's sarcophagus, and continued back to the site of the cave in. Bones set Rose on her feet, holding her at arm's length. "Princess, you with us?"

Rose nodded dully.

"Then up you go. Jessie, stay with her."

Nico went up the ladder next, followed by his two companions. The thump-thump of footfalls was getting louder with each passing second. Finally, it was Bones' turn. He started up the rungs but kept his eye on the passage until it was eclipsed from view. Even then, he didn't allow himself the luxury of sighing in relief.

He had just three rungs to go, when the king appeared below, stalking toward the ladder. Too impossibly big to scale it, the giant latched onto the bottom and with an almost disdainful effort, nearly ripped it from its moorings. Bones, realizing what was about to happen, scurried to the top and managed to get his hands on the lip of the pit, just in time to avoid a fatal tumble, but suddenly his lower half was swinging out into open air. Jessie wrapped both her hands around his right wrist, and Nico slid into view and snagged his left. Together, they pulled Bones to safety.

A tremor rippled through the ground. Bones glanced back to see a pair of impossibly large hands appear above the rim of the sinkhole, gripping the stone as he had done just a moment before.

Holy crap, Bones thought. *He just jumped thirty feet straight up.*

The stone crumbled under the weight of the creature and it disappeared from view, but Bones knew it would try again, and again, until it succeeded. He turned to Nico. "Will it follow us into town?"

"I don't know," Nico replied, though judging by his expression, Bones guessed it was a very real possibility.

"The last thing we want is to lead that thing into town," Bones said. "We'd be walking him right into the biggest all-you-can-eat buffet in history."

Nico pursed his lips together in thought for a moment—a moment that ended when another tremor signaled the giant's second attempt to jump up and climb out of the pit.

"Follow me," he said.

9

Nico led them through one of the nearby cemeteries and into an alley that ran behind the church. When they were able to slow to a walking pace, Bones caught up to the local man.

"What are we dealing with?" he asked in a hushed tone.

Nico was silent for a moment, considering the request, but then he relented. "He is the last of the Laestrygonians."

The name rang a bell for Bones, but Jessie was the one to make the connection. "You mean the giants from Homer's *Odyssey*?"

"The same, yes," Nico replied. "While exaggerated somewhat, they are just as ravenous as Homer described."

Jessie turned to Bones with a raised eyebrow.

"The Laestrygonians were a tribe of giants that supposedly occupied Sicily and Sardinia in ancient times. In the story they ate some of Odysseus' men on their way back to Ithaca," She looked at Nico. "They also threw boulders from the shore and destroyed a bunch of ships in his fleet, if I'm not mistaken."

Nico nodded. "You are correct." He went on, looking uncomfortable standing in one spot. "The king is the last of their kind now. If he dies, so does the race, and without a mate, that will eventually happen anyway."

"They never had kids?" Jessie asked.

"They did," Nico replied. "But that was a long

time ago."

"They died?" Bones asked.

Nico shook his head. "They ate them."

Jessie sucked her breath in, gagging a little, and even Bones felt faintly nauseated at this revelation.

"We think it is their natural behavior, like how a mother tiger might eat her young." He beckoned them to keep moving. "Without any access to the surface, they become agitated and hungry if not fed regularly. The first time my father attempted contact with the king, he was himself killed and his remains put on display like a trophy kill."

"Your father was eaten by the king?" Bones asked.

"I can still hear his screams in my sleep." His face softened. "I was only ten when it happened, almost thirty years ago now. It was the first time I was allowed access to their domain."

"That's awful," Jessie's voice quavered a little as she spoke.

Nico nodded.

Bones decided to ask the more pertinent question. "They can die. Can they be killed?"

Nico's look of uncertainty returned, but he nodded again.

"Then why didn't the townspeople go down there and clean house?"

"Leonardo…Mayor Giolito…felt it was our obligation to preserve the last of the Laestrygonians since it was his family that condemned them to death. He truly believes the giants to be gods among men."

"Condemned them to death? How so?"

"There have always been those in Cabras who

tended the Laestrygonians, provided them with food, which kept the people safe. They also kept people from exploring the tunnels where the giants had dwelt since ancient times. My grandfather and Leonardo's father were part of the secret order. Many years ago, however, a family sailed from the mainland and found a little-used cave entrance down by the water's edge and..." He shrugged. "The queen found them. You can imagine what happened."

"Ugh." Jessie said, looking like she was about to puke.

Bones was stunned.

"The sailboat was set adrift. What was left of the bodies was thrown into the sea. It was assumed that they fell overboard and were eaten by sharks." Nico shrugged again. "The outside world has never been interested in Cabras and my father, the mayor at the time, made sure no one ever looked too closely at us. But the incident caused great fear among the order. Some believed, as you probably do, that the time of the Laestrygonians was at an end. That they should be exterminated, so they dynamited the only tunnel large enough for them to escape, trapping them within. The order would continue to feed them, but they would never be allowed to hunt on the surface."

Bones shook his head. "If you had them trapped, why keep feeding them? You had a chance to end it?"

"I was only a child when it happened."

"That doesn't mean you're not partially responsible now," Bones said, his ire building. "You're obviously part of this order that... That worships these things."

Nico stopped and faced him. "Our families have

cared for the creatures for centuries. It is a tradition and an honor to do so."

"You're crazy," Jessie laughed.

Bones agreed with her reaction. It all sounded too unbelievable to be true. And, yet, here he was...

"Maybe you are right," Nico replied, nodding sadly. "Maybe we are insane."

"Is that why Mayor Giolito came back here?" Rose said, unexpectedly breaking her silence. She appeared to have recovered from the ordeal.

"It is," Nico confirmed. "When the last mayor was set to retire, he thought it best if someone knowledgeable of the situation ran things and we did not disagree. His power and influence have kept things quiet for a long time."

"Until the cave-in," Bones said. "Now the last of the giants is on the warpath."

Nico nodded solemnly. "This is our responsibility and we will end it.

They stopped again and peered out into the open road, looking back to the west. It was late, and the roads were empty, but there was no mistaking the extremely large naked figure standing at the edge of the sinkhole. Strangely, he did not appear to be looking for them or doing much of anything. He just stood there, statue still, facing west, towards the water with his arms out wide, head back as if enjoying the cool breeze. Bones realized that was probably exactly what he was doing, probably for the first time in a long time.

"Come," Nico urged, leading them across the street.

Everyone followed as quickly and as quietly as they could, but halfway across, Rose, stumbled and rolled her ankle. Yelping in both surprise and pain, she went down hard.

The giant's head snapped around, like a missile locking on target.

Bones reached back and made a furtive and ultimately futile grab for Rose's flailing hand.

"Hurry up!" Jessie whispered, trying to keep her voice down. "He's coming."

"Fantastic," Bones growled to himself, trying for Rose's hand again. Frustrated, he hissed at her. "Stop moving, dammit!"

Finally, he caught her wrist and pulled her into his arms, scrambling for cover behind a nearby parked truck. From this position, he could see Jessie and the others at the end of another alley, too far away to reach. Jessie made a patting gesture, then retreated from view. Bones intuitively grasped her meaning, and the urgency behind it, but even without the cue, he could tell from the tremors rippling through the ground that the giant was almost upon them.

Still hugging Rose in his arms, he ducked down and shifted to the far side of the truck where he dropped flat and looked under it. Two huge feet were visible on the opposite side, right next to the rear fender.

A strange scratchy sound filled the air. Sniffing. The king wasn't looking for them. He was trying to catch their scent.

Bad eyesight?

Bones pointed beneath the truck and thankfully Rose followed his orders without protest or question, easily sliding underneath. Being much bigger, Bones had to struggle to fit. His broad chest scraped the pavement as he squirmed into place, face down, alongside Rose.

There was another thump as the king dropped heavily to one knee. Bones could see a monstrous hand pressing against the road surface, fingers splayed, and heard the sniffing sound again. The king had their scent and was zeroing in on them. With a grunt, the giant lowered his massive head down even lower.

Then Bones heard a different sound, a softer hiss like someone spraying....

Perfume!

A cloying floral aroma hit his olfactory senses like a sledgehammer. He turned his head to the side and saw Rose hurriedly squeezing the atomizer bulb of a small crystal vial. A cloud of mist issued from the bottle with each squeeze, the fine droplets settling onto both off them.

The king sniffed again and then made a strangled sound which culminated in a thunderous sneeze that showered Rose in ropy strands of mucous.

Way to go, Rose, Bones thought, impressed.

The gigantic head vanished as the king got back to his feet, but the sneezes continued. Then, after a few seconds—and just as many sneezes—the giant's feet disappeared from view as well. The primordial creature didn't know what to make of it, but he did understand one thing, whatever it was, wasn't edible.

Bones wormed closer to the edge of the truck and could just make out the shape of the giant, stomping back to the west, back towards the cave-in. The hunt was seemingly over, and Bones had the most unlikely person to thank for saving his life.

"Nice work, Rose," he said, wiggling free from beneath the truck. He reached down and helped her up. "Looks like you're more than just good looks and attitude."

Something struck his arm from behind and he jumped, startled.

"Hitting on my friend, are we?"

For once in his life, Bones was caught with nothing to say. Then he realized that both Jessie and Rose were laughing, and his cheeks flushed. He was spared further embarrassment when Nico emerged from the alley and came over to shake his hand. Then, he leaned into Bones and sniffed, looking very confused, but after a moment he shook his head. "Where is the king?"

Bones jerked a thumb over his shoulder. "He took his ball and went home."

Nico's eyes widened. "Vivianna and the others are still down there! Trapped! You must help me free them!"

Bones shrugged. "There's nothing we can do for them right now. What about that other entrance? Can they get out through there?"

"No, it is impassable. The only other way out is through the entrance under city hall, and that path will take them through where the giant lives."

Bones could only close his eyes and sigh. "Talk about a rock and a hard place," he grumbled. "And you want us to get in there with them."

"Bones?" Jessie said. "You know we have to help, right?"

He relented. "Yeah, yeah, I know."

Nico turned to his brothers and quickly said something in Italian. Without a reply, the two men took off the other way. Nico turned back to Bones and Jessie. "They are going to the hidden entrance to keep watch."

Bones raised a curious eyebrow. "And where are we going?"

"One cannot fight a war without weapons, no?"

"Weapons?" Bones asked.

"When I was a young man, I was in the Italian Army. I may have taken a few things home with me for, how do you say, 'a rainy day.'"

As they followed Nico through the streets of Cabras, Bones took a good, long look at the man. A stout, thick Italian who had what looked like a forever-five-o'clock shadow. He possessed hairy arms that seemed a few inches too long for his frame and broad shoulders. He sort of looked gorilla-like from behind, and based on their first meeting, Bones would have assumed he was nothing more than that—the town muscle, a bully. But now Nico was revealing a different side of himself, a willingness to take action to save others, despite being scared out of his mind. That was something Bones could appreciate.

10

"Holy crap, Nico! Holy. Freaking. Crap."

Beneath the floorboards of Nico and Vivianna's apartment above the restaurant were three long containers about the size of guitar cases, but the one Bones opened contained something a little more powerful than a Fender *Stratocaster*.

"I feel like Antonio Banderas!"

"I loved *Mask of Zorro!*" Nico exclaimed.

"I liked him as *Puss in Boots*," Jessie added.

Bones closed his eyes, deflated. "Just drop it. I really don't want to shoot either of you."

Jessie and Nico just stared at him, still not understanding the reference or his irritated reaction.

"*El Mariachi*? Guitar case full of guns? Any of this ring a bell?"

Heads shook.

"Neither of you have heard of *Desperado*?"

They both shrugged.

He rolled his eyes and returned his attention to the weapon in his hands.

The Franchi SPAS-15 resembled an assault rifle, but was in fact a semi-automatic shotgun. Next to it were four Berretta 92FS pistols. Bones took two of the handguns along with four extra mags. One gun, along with two mags, went to Jessie, who looked a little unsure. Nevertheless, she accepted the weapon and additional ammo, ready to roll.

Not that the 9mm rounds will do anything, he

thought, recalling how they only pissed off the king earlier. *Still... They're better than nothing.*

Looking very comfortable with his Berretta ARX 160 assault rifle, Nico opened the third and final case. Inside was an assortment of stuff, including holsters, grenades, and several packets of Semtex plastic explosives.

"Take it all," Bones said, pointing to the mustard-colored bricks. "If we can't kill the king, we'll need to bury him deep."

Bones glanced at Rose who quietly sat in the corner of the room, knees to her chest. She was staying on her own decision. Bones didn't even have to tell her to.

He looked back at Nico. "Anything else you can tell us about them? They don't see well from what I can tell."

He nodded. "A lifetime of darkness has made his eyesight poor, but his other senses are better than yours or mine. Unfortunately, I have not been able to acquire anything in the way of night vision equipment."

"It means we'll have to be extra careful when on his home turf," Bones replied. "Topside, he's a sitting duck, out of his element. But down there..." He didn't need to finish. Nico understood better than anyone.

"What happens to Cabras after this is over?" Jessie asked. "Will the mayor resign since there isn't anything to protect anymore?"

"You think Giolito will want that even if this threat is neutralized?" Bones was honestly curious.

"Why wouldn't he?" Nico asked.

"In my experience, men with power will do anything to stay in power. If after Cabras is saved and becomes a normal town, what happens if someone more qualified and better-connected runs against Giolito in the next election?"

"He's in total control right now," Jessie added. "He'd lose that control if all this vanishes."

Nico didn't look like he was buying it but the look on his face gave away that he was at least considering it. "So, you are saying Leonardo would rather have this creature remain over his town's future?"

"And safety," Jessie added.

"Who says he'd tell anyone?" Bones said. "If I were him, I'd continue to do things the same way. He'd only have your family to persuade. You may not be with him but are your brothers? What about your wife—*his* sister?"

Nico sneered. "I know Vivianna well enough to know she wants that thing dead. If Leonardo tries to turn her against me…" He didn't finish. Instead, he shouldered the pack full of explosives. Nico was ready to move.

"You have any rope?" Bones asked, thinking as he spoke.

Nico nodded, nostrils flared.

"Good, because we now lack most of a ladder thanks to our new friend."

Nico left the room, giving Bones a moment with Jessie.

"You don't have to do this," he said to her, honestly a little afraid for her. "Rose probably wouldn't mind the company."

For a moment, she looked relieved by the offer, but then her expression hardened, and she stood tall. "I'm fine."

He grinned. "Yes… Yes, you are."

"God…" She looked at Nico as he reentered the room, coiled rope in hand. "Do Italian soldiers act like this before going out on a mission?"

Nico shook his head. "Didn't think so."

Bones grinned again, accepting the offered rope. "Ain't nobody like me but me."

They exited quietly down the rear stairs and headed back to the dig site.

Circling around from the south, Bones and Nico led the way while Jessie, handgun gripped tightly, brought up the rear. It was the same path they'd taken earlier that day. Now, close to midnight, the streets were empty, the town silent. Bones could hear the gentle breeze over the water to the west, giving him an idea.

"Can they swim?"

Nico looked at him. "What?"

"The king…can the giants swim? I don't remember reading that they could."

Nico shrugged. "I don't think so. It would make sense if they could not, though. Homer's *Odyssey* said they stayed on shore and hurled large rocks into the water."

"Sure sounds like they can't," Jessie commented. She'd been silent since leaving Nico's place. "If they could, they probably would've just swam out to the ships and finished them off."

Plan B, Bones thought. But he wasn't so sure they'd be able to lure him out to sea.

They slowly crept up to the pit and peeked over the precipice. The ladder to Bones' surprise was still somewhat intact. Its uppermost anchors were still attached to the ground above. The base of the ladder was what was ripped free during the king's assault. After thirty seconds of waiting and watching, Bones unfurled the rope and tied off an end around the closest light post he could find. He'd use the ladder until he couldn't. Cautiously, he made his way below.

"The ladder is still strong enough to hold," Bones said, halfway down. Then, it creaked. He looked up. "For now…"

Once down, Bones covered the entrance to the tunnel while Jessie and Nico joined him one at a time. There, they knelt and listened, just in case the giant was near and waiting for them.

After a tense moment of nothing, Bones stood and started into the passage, lighting their way with the tactical flashlight mounted to the rails of the SPAS-15. Nico's rifle was similarly equipped, and Jessie carried Bones' Maglite. She also kept the pistol drawn, but down next to her thigh.

"In we go," Bones muttered.

"Creepy, huh?" Jessie whispered. The still air making her soft words sound like they had been shouted.

Bones shrugged. "It's not *that* bad." He glanced over at Jessie who had a horrified look on her face. "What?" he asked. "I'm terribly desensitized, you know."

Even though he meant it in jest, he realized it was the actual truth. Things like this felt pretty normal to him now and he wasn't sure if that was a good or bad thing.

He tried for something more inspiring. "If it bleeds, we can kill it."

That got a reply out of Nico. "Predator, very good. I read about that film in the *Schwarzenegger Presidential Library*."

"Huh?" Jessie said. "Arnold wasn't the—"

Bones smiled. "It's from *Demolition Man.*" He nodded, as they entered the second tomb, impressed. "My man has good taste in movies… Even if he doesn't know who *El Mariachi* is."

"If you two don't shut up," Jessie hissed, "I'll have to *lick* your asses."

They both stopped and turned. Jessie's expression was defiant. "See," she said, "I know Stallone movies too. My mind just happens to be on something else. I'm sorry I don't know who the guitar case guy is. Sue me for being a baby when these movies came out!"

Bones held up his hand for her to calm down and couldn't help himself. "Okay, look, just do me a favor and," his eyes shot to Nico, "take a moment and *be well.*"

Nico tried in vain to hold back laughter.

Jessie put the gun under her armpit and rubbed her face with both hands. "Ugh, someone put me back in the fridge…"

That got a laugh from both men and Jessie soon joined in. With the *Demolition Man* quotes out of the way, and a little of the tension lessened, they continued toward the queen's burial chamber.

A guttural roar echoed around them, freezing them in place. Bones responded by tightening the shotgun to his shoulder. Nico spun to watch their rear, putting Jessie in between himself and Bones.

Then, nothing. It was as quiet as before.

"Where is he?" Jessie asked.

"The sound. It seems to come from everywhere," Nico replied.

They moved on, passing the dead man and continuing to the entry to the throne room. A few fires still lit the large space, but most were nothing more than scattered cinders.

"Someone seems slightly miffed," Bones muttered under his breath.

Jessie stepped up next to him. "Well, at least we know which way he went."

"He is not used to his prey escaping him," Nico said from behind. Bones and Jessie turned. "We must be extra careful."

"Thanks for telling us *now*, Nicky," Bones said, facing the room again.

Bones inhaled deeply and picked up on a scent that he didn't like. While the room was filled with the bones of the dead and a thick blanket of smoke, it wasn't either of those that he smelled, it was him, or rather, Rose's perfume. Would the king remember that scent? If so, how would he react?

Nothing I can do about it now.

After scanning the room, Bones quickly descended the giant-sized stairs to the bottom, the others following right behind him.

"See anyone?" Jessie asked quietly.

Bones knew what she meant. This was where they had left Santi, Giolito, and Vivianna to face the king's rage. Even though he knew it was the right thing to do at the time, he still felt bad about leaving them behind.

He shook his head.

After a quick survey of the room, Nico started up the east steps.

"Are we even sure they went that way?" Bones asked, looking for a trail to follow. The king had scattered bones all over the previously cleared paths encircling the throne, making it next to impossible to tell which paths had been trod.

"Yes," Nico replied, confident. "They know that the only way out is east beneath city hall. It's how we came in."

"What about the dig site?" Bones asked, confused. He knelt and wiped his hand across the floor.

"No. They know better than to follow behind him."

Bones looked back up the north and south tunnels, still unsure. "And those?" He glanced over his shoulder to Nico. "They go anywhere we should know about?"

Nico shook his head. "The northern tunnel is the one we collapsed to trap the Laestrygonians underground. The south leads around to the east, bypassing the giant's domain, but it is a long and difficult passage. The quickest route back to safety is the one we have always used, even though it means going through the giant's home."

"Tell me about the eastern exit," Bones said.

"It is man-made," Nico said. "My father helped build it—too small for a giant to fit through. They broke through rock beneath city hall and built a hidden entrance below, so that we could minister to the needs of the Laestrygonians."

"What can we expect when we get there?" Bones asked.

Nico's face fell. "It is probably better that you see it with your own eyes."

Bones eyed Jessie who shrugged.

Satisfied with the half-explanation, Bones moved to the foot of the eastern staircase and immediately found what he was looking for. A set of large disturbances could be seen in the bones in front of the first step. The giant had most definitely come this way, crushing the skeletal remains beneath his feet, but he also saw smaller prints mixed in, carrying the dust along with them.

"East it is."

11

The remaining trek to the king's lair was uneventful—which was exactly what Bones hoped for. Secondary tunnels broke off from the main one, revealing more tombs and alcoves, looking very similar to the tunnels behind them. The tombs, thankfully, held sarcophagi and not recent kills. The alcoves were what might have been additional places of worship or possibly secondary dining rooms but some of the passages simply led off into the unknown depths of the cavern system.

Good thing we've got Nico along, Bones thought, moving his light back and forth as he walked. *If we get turned around, we could be lost down here for hours. Maybe even days.*

"We should be close."

Nico's comment brought Bones' mind back and he nodded his response.

"You see that?" Jessie's voice was a scared quaver.

Just ahead of them, the tunnel seemed to be glowing red. If the king's lair was anything like his throne room, Bones guessed it was also lit by firelight. The air had become increasingly warm, and smoke whorled around them.

"Stay quiet and stay ready," he urged in a low voice. "Gonna be damn hot in there," he added, mostly to himself.

"Yes," Nico agreed. "The creatures prefer the warmth of their fires over the cool air coming off the sea."

Maybe we can extinguish a few of the fires, cool this place down enough to draw him to the surface.

Bones continued forward slowly until the passage opened up, giving him his first look at the lair of the Laestrygonian king. "Son of a…"

Lair wasn't the right word for what he beheld. *City* was a better fit. It was truly a necropolis—a "city of the dead."

"This is where it lives?" Jessie asked, breathless.

Like the throne room, the ceiling continued on, only rising slightly in elevation. And like the throne room, the floor sunk away, disappearing beneath mountains of bones and car-sized fire pits. The large-stepped staircase was similar to the throne room's too, except it was twice as long. It was at least fifty or sixty vertical feet to the paths that led through the city itself. The fires within raged so hot and bright that Bones could see the entire cavern from one side to the other.

A hellish radiance that looked like a rolling lava flow was visible along the north and south edge of the immense chamber. Whatever the source, the radiant heat coming off it would probably be enough to snuff out the life of anyone or anything who venture too close.

Note to self…avoid the north and south walls.

Putting out a couple of fires wasn't going to make a bit of difference. There were just too damn many of them for that to work.

There were several structures on the floor of the cavern, similar in style to Grecian temples, but scaled up in size for the Laestrygonians. Even from a distance, Bones could see the columns and the ornate gable they supported were made of stone… and bone. He could even see a few of them sticking out of each of the supports.

There were four smaller temples surrounding it, all solidly built, and equally spaced around the central structure like the pips on the five-side of an ordinary die.

"Who built all this?" Jessie asked.

"That is something we do not know," Nico softly replied. "The first time my ancestors came down here, this was already here. We know it is old and obviously made for the Laestrygonians, but as far as who actually built it or when... The giants did not keep records, unfortunately."

"Doesn't matter," Bones said, standing. "I take it the only way out is through?"

Nico nodded.

"Let's hope we don't run into His Majesty." He made his way down. "Keep an eye out for the others too. We may not get a ton of time to search."

"I thought we were here to kill it," Jessie said, holding up her gun.

"Bullets didn't cut it last time," Bones countered, recalling how little the Glock did. "Maybe our combined firepower can do the trick in round two, but I wouldn't count on it. The best thing we can hope for is to bury this place and starve him."

"That's terrible," she said.

Bones shrugged. "I don't like it either, but if it's him or us, I'm choosing us ten out of ten times. I like being alive."

"Agreed," Nico said.

Like the throne room, there were bones everywhere, but many of the skeletons were still at least partly articulated. Also, instead of the remains being strewn about like trash, some of the bodies seemed to be on display like trophies.

Giant skulls were impaled on spikes. Others were placed above sarcophagi.

"The royal family and their enemies," Nico said, seeing Bones' peaked curiosity. "The king and queen's direct bloodline would eventually be laid to rest here—as were their rivals.

"Rivals?" Jessie asked.

"Yes," Nico replied. "Their heads are the ones pierced with spikes."

"There were more tribes than the king's here?" Bones asked.

Nico nodded. "A long time ago, yes."

"Tell me more about the rival tribes," Bones said.

"As I am sure you have determined, the tunnels below run beneath all of Sardinia. This was not the only clan of Laestrygonians that survived into modern times."

Bones took a second to contemplate what he just heard. Exhaling, he spoke. "Looks like we dodged a major bullet then. Could you imagine if we came down here during their heyday?"

"I'll have to show you my order's records," Nico said, like it was no big deal. "They tried to come here a few hundred years ago and were almost completely wiped out."

How many of these things were there?" Bones asked himself.

"Why was the queen's body up top and not here?" Jessie asked.

"It is customary for them to be buried above until their spots here are readied."

"Is that where the queen's body is now?" Bones asked.

Nico nodded. "We brought it here shortly before you discovered it missing. It is in there." He pointed at the largest temple.

"How do you all move around here freely?" Jessie asked, keeping the conversation on the present and not the past.

"He knows we worship him and provide him with sustenance."

"The king understands you?" Bones asked.

"I am not sure to be honest with you. The queen seemed to, though. I think he understands our physical posturing, bowing, chanting. Plus, we never came armed and never posed any real threat to them. Why would he fear us now?"

A cleared path broke off to one of the smaller temples, it too was lined with fire on both sides. Waves of heat roiled the air before them. Bones was already soaked with sweat, his t-shirt sticking to his arms, back, and chest. The smoke-filled air wasn't helping things either. Breathing was becoming more and more cumbersome with every step taken. It felt like he was moving through a pizza oven.

He glanced down to Jessie. "You okay?"

She nodded and peeled her hair from her forehead. "But it's getting hard to breathe."

"Stay low," he said. "The air won't be as bad down there."

Jessie lowered herself even more and sighed. She closed her eyes and breathed normally. "Heat…rises," she said in between breaths. "Smoke, too."

"Whenever you need air," Bones instructed, "find a place to hide and duck down to the ground."

Another roar echoed through the chamber. They

all froze, weapons up.

"That came from the king's temple," Nico whispered. "He is home."

Squinting through the haze, Bones beheld the largest of the temples in the center of the cavern. Now that they were down at floor level, he understood just how enormous it was.

The columns were as thick as redwoods and almost as tall. Each was spaced out twenty feet from the other. The sinister mix of stone and bone was sickening to look at, but it showed off the builder's macabre ingenuity.

"Stay focused," he told himself.

Something moved amidst the miasma and judging by the size of the disruption, Bones knew it was the king. Yet, strangely, the movements didn't appear to be rage-fueled. If anything, the giant looked almost sad.

Curious despite himself, Bones left the path and crept carefully across the bone pile toward the king's temple. Jessie and Nico followed without comment or complaint.

The heat grew so intense that he had to shield his face against it with his forearm.

When he reached the edge of the temple, he leaned around a column and peered inside. At chest height, the interior was easy for him to see. He watched as the king paced back and forth, growling incoherently to himself. After a moment of watching, Bones saw why.

There was an altar at the center of the temple and lying atop it was an enormous humanoid-shape wrapped in linens.

"It's her," Jessie whispered. "It's the queen."

12

The altar was not an altar, Bones saw, but a sort of cot or bed, with strips of pale hide stretched across the frame. Bones instantly recognized the "leather" as skin.

Human skin.

Ugh.

Leaning another six inches to his right, he saw that the king was not alone. Mayor Giolito, Dr. Santi and Vivianna were there too, sitting on the floor, huddled together in fear. None of them were tied up or immobilized in any way.

Why would they be? Bones knew they had nowhere to go if they ran.

Giolito was pleading in Italian, and strangely, the giant seemed to be listening.

"Is he…talking…to him?" Jessie asked.

"Looks like it," Bones replied, leaning back to look at Nico.

Nico quietly translated for the Americans. "He says, 'We are sorry! We only moved her so she would not be found.'"

Bones nodded thoughtfully, realizing that there was more to the king's rage than mere hunger.

The giant stopped and pounded a foot into the stone flooring, cracking it.

Holy crap!

Then, the king spoke, using a language that Bones had never heard before. It sounded like a mix of Italian and caveman grunts. Certain words were familiar—Bones spoke a little gutter Spanish and there were some similarities between that and Italian, but most of it sounded like gobbledygook.

But the mayor understood it just fine.

Nico again translated his reply, "No, my king, we did not mean to anger you."

"It…understands…Italian?" Jessie asked.

Understanding the language was interesting in itself but the fact the giant could somewhat vocalize a response was even more interesting. The Laestrygonian king was smart and he'd been taught.

Bones looked back out over the subterranean city, finally seeing the truth. The Laestrygonians had built this city themselves. They weren't mindless brutes but intelligent creatures. A unique species already doomed to extinction.

"We must act now," Nico said, raising his rifle.

"Woah there." Bones gently pushed the barrel of the weapon back down. "We need a plan first. Gotta be careful to not get anyone killed."

Nico didn't respond, barely even looking at him. At the moment, he only cared about getting his wife out in one piece. He was ready to go to war.

Bones briefly outlined his plan for rescuing the hostages, and, this time, he got a nod of understanding from Nico.

"Right," Bones said, "let's do this."

Bones rolled to his left and Nico to his right. Together, they quickly scaled the large steps, leaping up onto the temple platform in unison.

"Nobody move!" Bones shouted, looking over the barrel of his shotgun.

All four of the temple's occupants turned their

attention towards him and Nico. Three were relieved to see the armed men. One, however, wasn't so happy.

The giant faced them and sneered. Then, he began speaking—hollering—at Bones, spittle flying as he did. Bones replied with a loud noise of his own, firing the shotgun into the air with the hopes of at least frightening the king with his boom stick.

It didn't work.

Instead of fleeing, the giant charged. Bones quickly snapped the barrel down and sent more buckshot flying. It ate into the creature's thigh, stumbling it some. The wound exploded with blood, and yet, the king stayed on his feet.

"Now, Nico. Go!"

Bones saw Nico go sprinting out of his field of vision. The latter yelled for the others to move as he did. At least, Bones thought that's what he said. It was in Italian after all.

Bones rolled to the right, but in his exhausted, dehydrated state, he struggled to complete the maneuver. Firing from his knee, he clipped the king in the side, earning another retort from the monster, but once again, the creature refused to go down. Stunned at his heavy-hitting weapon's ineffectiveness, all Bones could do was backpedal and match the limping giant's pace.

Grunting, the king quickened his steps. Bones responded by squeezing off three more shots before turning and running. He didn't know if any of them found their mark, the giant's roars suggested that at least one of them did. Bones headed south hoping to keep the thing busy long enough for Nico to get the others clear.

He leaped from the raised platform and landed hard, barely staying on his feet. He looked over his shoulder and watched in awe as the giant burst through one of the mighty columns. Bone and stone went sailing into the air, like thick pieces of shrapnel peppering the spot where he'd last seen Jessie.

Dammit.

The heat was even more oppressive to the south, but that was the least hellish thing he encountered as he sprinted toward the south wall. Between the temple and the edge of the cave was a forest of crucifixions. Hundreds of corpses had been tied, spread-eagled, to X-shaped crosses and staked out to mummify in the heat.

The first ones he encountered were recent kills. They had been skinned but otherwise left intact. Each and every one of them had looks of terror on their faces. They'd been alive when made into trophies...

There were items of discarded clothing strewn about—shirts and hats alike.

The missing crew members?

There were seven bodies in all. Added to the one they had found in the tunnels and that made eight.

The Laestrygonian king had killed them all.

That solves one of the mysteries.

He darted past them, and continued down the row, passing leathery corpses. Most were completely desiccated—filleted alive.

The southern edge of the cavern was a furnace, a long stone trough of pure heat. Flaming cinders erupted from it at random intervals. Up close, at least as close as Bones dared to get, it looked like nothing less than a river of magma under a volcano.

And it was between him and the exit.

Bones charged forward and leaped out over the flaming trough.

Should'a probably thought this through a little more, he thought, as the heat felt like it had scorched his body down to his bones.

But the super-heated air seemed to lift him up, buoying him along as he arced over the furnace to the narrow, cinder-strew walk on the far side. Landing hard, Bones rolled and hurried away from the scalding heat. As he scrambled back to his feet, he looked back to see the king standing on the opposite side, pacing back and forth as if trying to decide whether to dare the flames as Bones had done.

Bones decided to give the monster something else to worry about. He shouldered the shotgun and unloaded the remainder of the magazine at the furious creature. Two of the shot loads hit the giant in the gut, knocking him away. Bones bolted to the right, running along the walkway as, across the flames, the king tried to regain his footing. He got more than halfway to the end of the trough before he heard the giant's telltale roar.

Come on legs, don't fail me now.

Bones was a natural runner, and his years as a SEAL had further developed his ability to endure in even the worst imaginable situations. Unfortunately, this situation was beyond anyone's wildest imagination. He was exhausted, dehydrated, slowly baking to death, and to top it all off, his back was killing him.

Directly ahead, the walkway narrowed into a ledge and then ended altogether, the furnace trough curling around it to meet the cavern wall. Across the searing flames, he could see the giant pounding forward with his immense strides, easily closing on him.

"Damn, damn, damn," he rasped, reaching down for one last all-out push. It was going to be close.

He judged the number of steps it would take to reach the end of the ledge, visualizing exactly where each footfall would land, and shortened his stride a little so that his final step would place his back leg almost exactly on the precipice. When he got there—his estimate damn near perfect—he launched himself once more out over the fiery trough. Flames licked at him, and suddenly he felt a bloom of intense heat searing the skin of his chest. As a horrible smell filled his nostrils, he realized what had happened—his T-shirt had ignited.

And then, he was through it. The ground rose up to him, but this time, the giant was right there. As before, he didn't try to land on his feet, but threw himself to the side, rolling his body right into the onrushing giant.

It felt like hitting a tree. The impact drove the hot breath from his scorched lungs. But from the corner of his eye, he saw the giant stumbling away. The blow had taken the king's legs out from under him, and as he flailed about trying to recover his footing, he went crashing into the forest of crucified skeletons.

As he overcame the initial daze of impact, Bones remembered catching on fire. He frantically ripped off his scorched T-shirt. His landing roll had snuffed out the flames, and thankfully, the burns felt like nothing more than hot spots on his skin—first degree, at the very worst.

Scrambling back to his feet, he began looking for the giant and found him squirming beneath an entanglement of bones and broken crosses. It took him a moment longer to realize that the giant wasn't going to be chasing after him any time soon. The creature's right leg looked like raw hamburger, and a large splinter of wood was lodged in his side. Blood streamed from those wounds and many others as he unsuccessfully struggled to free himself.

Bones jammed the shotgun into the crook of his shoulder, as he stalked towards the trapped monster.

Careful to keep a safe standoff distance, he aimed the weapon at the giant's face and curled his finger around the trigger. At this range, the blast would take of most, if not, all of the enormous head.

But Bones didn't pull the trigger.

"Can you understand me?"

The Laestrygonian stopped what he was doing and stared at Bones. His breath was coming in ragged gasps, but after a moment, his head cocked to the side. Bones doubted the giant could comprehend English, but he knew it understood verbal communication, so figured it was worth a try. He really didn't want to kill the last of a species—any species. So, instead, he was going to give the creature an ultimatum.

He lowered the weapon so that it was no longer pointing directly at the giant and spoke slowly. "I'm leaving now. If you try to come after me, I'll blow your friggin' head off." When the giant did not respond, Bones relaxed his aim further. "Frankly, I don't give a rat's ass whether you live or die. But I'd just as soon not be the one to cross you off the endangered species list. I've got enough on my conscience and don't need Hagrid's death on it, too."

Satisfied that he'd gotten his point across, Bones turned away…

Just as the king snarled and ripped free of the makeshift snare.

So much for that idea.

Bones, half-expecting the treacherous reversal,

wheeled and brought the shotgun up, squeezing the trigger as the giant clawed wildly at him.

Nothing happened.

The weapon was empty.

"Crap!"

Before Bones could further berate himself for making such a rookie mistake, a sweep of the giant's hand struck the useless shotgun from his grasp, sending it flying. Diving forward to avoid the follow-up attack, Bones crashed through one of the ancient crucifixions. The brittle wood and bone exploded into a cloud of dust and Lord only knew what else. Trying not to think about what—or who—he was inhaling, Bones scrambled forward, narrowly avoiding another swipe from the enraged giant.

He thought about drawing his Berretta but decided against it. The 9mm rounds would probably only piss the giant off ever further, and right now, having his hands free was a lot more important. He needed to get back across the bone field, find Jessie and Nico, and get clear of the underground city so they could blow the tunnel entrance and permanently trap the king underground.

He looked over his shoulder and watched as the king bashed his way through the morbid display. The giant seemed to be moving slower than before, but he was still covering ground almost as fast as Bones.

He veered off in the direction of the temple, towards the now broken section left by the king's exit. There, beneath a pile of rubble, was Jessie. She was out cold and bleeding from a head wound. Not having time to check the injury's severity, Bones hefted her over his left shoulder and set off on a steady but awkward pace down the path back to the throne room.

He paused at the foot of the steps, gazing up at the long ascent that lay between him and freedom. "Man, I hate stairs," he grumbled.

But then another howling roar from the king, much too close for comfort, changed his mind. "Well, maybe they're not *that* bad."

13

The stairs, which had been built to accommodate the longer legs of the Laestrygonians, were just as awful as he originally thought. Jessie, slung over his shoulder in a fireman's carry, didn't weigh a lot, but he was so depleted that every additional pound felt like a hundred. He felt like he was climbing an escalator made of quicksand moving in the wrong direction.

The king let out another roar, buffeting Bones like the hot wind off the furnace. He was close, so close that Bones didn't even dare look. But an ember of defiance still glowed within him.

"Shut the hell up, bro!" he shouted—or tried to. It came out as more of a series of rasping grunts. "If I want a comment from the peanut gallery I'll ask, thank you very much!"

Jessie mumbled something in his ear.

Good. She was coming to. Maybe she'd be able to walk on her own. Too bad he couldn't stop even for the second or two it would take to set her down.

"What?" He leaned in closer to her face.

She repeated what she said.

"Good one…"

Bones grinned. "I have my moments.".

He reached flat ground a few steps later and dashed into the dark passage. He smiled when the tunnel lit up in the aura of a familiar light. Despite the awkwardness of her perch, Jessie had the wherewithal to turn on her Maglite.

"Thanks," he said.

With the path lit and the temperature dropping, Bones got his second wind and continued ahead at a slow jog.

When he was sure that the king was falling further behind, he paused long enough to set Jessie down, and after making sure that she was more or less able to stay on her own feet, they started running again. Unfortunately, the king also seemed to catch his second wind.

They had just reached the center of the throne room, and were preparing for one more torturous ascent, when the king emerged from the east entrance behind them.

They bounded up the steps, sprinted past the alcoves and through the burial chambers, passing the partially consumed remains of the graduate student. Bones could feel the cool night air on his face, telling him they were close.

But then, as they ran out of the queen's burial chamber, Jessie's foot caught one of the extinguished stand lights. She stumbled and fell, crashing into Bones, and taking him out too. Flailing to regain their balance, they half-tumbled through the passage and finally skidded to a stop in the main excavation pit, gazing up into the calm night sky above Sardinia.

"Come…on…" he panted.

Grabbing Jessie's feeble hand, he hauled her to the ladder. She needed to scale it herself, though. He'd never admit it aloud, but Bones wasn't sure he had enough energy left to pull her up with him. Plus, the ladder was in no shape to hold them both at the same time. It had barely held Bones by himself.

The beast's roar was close and reverberated

through the tunnel, smacking Bones right in the face. Jessie cursed and started climbing, but she was moving slow. Too slow.

"Move that sweet ass! We have incoming!"

He drew his pistol, leveled it at the passageway, and waited, checking on Jessie's progress every few seconds. When she was halfway up, he went against his better judgement, slid the gun into his jeans at the small of his back, and then mounted the ladder to begin his own climb. The giant arrived a few moments later, stalking over and grabbing at Bones' dangling foot.

On his third attempt, the giant caught it and squeezed. Bones recalled how easily the giant had crushed the stone at the edge of the cave-in and waited for him to do the same to his ankle. Panicking, Bones latched on tighter with his hands and released his free foot, dangling fifteen feet above the ground. Looking between his legs, he started slamming his free foot into the king's face. In between blows, he noticed that the giant was only using one hand. The other was clutching his badly bleeding side. The repeated blows broke the giant's nose, shaking him loose and spilling him back until he crashed into the sarcophagus.

The impact knocked the lid askew, and it slid off to reveal a skeleton of a being even larger than the one beneath Bones—easily twelve feet tall, despite being reduced to nothing but bones.

But there was no time to study this amazing discovery. Bones quickly climbed the rest of the way up, favoring his now throbbing right ankle as he did.

His eyes widened when the ladder creaked, then buckled. The top moorings, the only ones still attached to the wall, were about to come loose and drop him. He struggled to grasp the rope that dangled off to his left, missing it as the ladder sagged away from the wall.

Clawing his way up, he was startled when Jessie reached out for his wrists, just as the ladder ripped free and plummeted into the excavation.

"I can't… hold you," she said between grunts.

Bones pulled his left hand free and latched onto the rope. He found a foothold, pushed with his good leg, and, along with Jessie's help, practically launched himself out of the hole. They fell away from the edge of the excavation and crashed to the ground.

Jessie landed on his chest, almost knocking the wind out of him. He groaned from the impact and she quickly sat up, smiling.

"I just noticed something."

"What?" he croaked.

"Where's your shirt?"

Still on his back, he pointed to the cave-in. "Back in the hole. Burned it up pretty good back there."

Jessie huffed. "Well, at least you made it out on your feet. I had to be carried."

He stood and helped her to her feet. "At least you had a half-naked hunk to cling too."

Bones picked up his felled weapon and slowly made his way to the edge of the cave-in. He didn't want to get any closer than he had to, but he needed to know what happened with the king. He put a finger to his lips and motioned for Jessie to stay back. She too held her gun firmly and stepped out to his right for a better angle. The last thing either of them needed was for Bones to get a bullet in the back—from Jessie no less.

Another step.

Come on.

Another step.

Dammit, show yourself.

Another step.

Um…maybe he left?

One more step and he'd be able to see most of the pit. He could already see a third of it and the giant was nowhere to be found. Bones prayed that the giant had decided to cut his losses and retreat.

Bones leaned over the edge….

And was clubbed to the side.

He took the shot to his left shoulder and attempted to roll out of it, but instead landed on a chunk of something in the ground. Whatever it was jabbed him in the back hard enough to make him gasp for air, halting his movements.

The next thing he knew, the beaten and bloodied Laestrygonian king was standing above him teeth bared, snarling like a rabid dog. Jessie opened up with her pistol. The 9mm rounds bit into his skin but did little else. The king only had to raise his thick arm and block the bullets from hitting anything vital.

After her mag ran dry, Bones knew he was done for.

The king raised his clenched fist, looked Bones square in the eyes, and brought it down like a guillotine. With inches to spare, the giant halted his deathblow at a sound that Bones recognized. Somewhere behind him tires screeched, protesting their owner's sudden stop. Doors popped, and men shouted. With his attention elsewhere now, Bones slowly inched away from the still dangerous beast.

He winced when his jeans scraped against gravel. The king looked his way once more and growled but then the air was filled with the thunder of automatic weapons. The giant staggered back, buffeted by the attack. Bones rolled away, landing on his belly, facing his rescuers. Nico, and the two men from before, his brothers, all had their weapons trained on the agitated monster. Behind them was a black Mercedes SUV. Its windows were down, giving Bones a look at its occupants.

Dr. Santi, Mayor Giolito, and Vivianna were jammed into the back seat.

Bones turned to face the giant, who seethed with rage, blood and saliva draining down his chin as he snarled and shouted what could only be Laestrygonian obscenities.

Not wanting to give the king a third chance to squish him like a bug, Bones scrambled to his feet and headed for the three gunmen, but then a crazy plan came to him. He shifted direction and went for the SUV instead.

Nico gave him a questioning look, but Bones hardly paid him any attention. His focus was on the vehicle. As he climbed in, he looked into the rearview mirror and simply said, "Out."

Santi and Vivianna immediately threw open their doors and slid out, but a still-sweat-soaked Giolito defiantly crossed his arms and locked eyes with Bones in the mirror.

Grunting, Bones turned and faced the man. "Either you get out, or you become a permanent addition to this site."

Giolito's stare wavered slightly. For an extra kick in the ass, Bones shifted the SUV into *drive*. In time with the click of the transmission, Giolito's eyebrows arched and his nostrils flared. The man was furious and for a moment, Bones thought he would call the bluff.

And it was a bluff. Bones wouldn't have sacrificed Giolito's life to kill the giant. But before he could come up with a better solution, the mayor opened his door and slid out.

Problem solved.

Bones cranked the wheel and floored the gas pedal, stomping on it hard. The same screeching sound he had heard before erupted beneath him as the SUV's wheels spun. When they caught, it and Bones were thrown forward off the main road in the direction of the excavation.

He blared the horn, getting Nico and the others to move. They parted, diving out of the way and giving him a direct line to the king. Bones kept the SUV's trajectory straight and true and initiated phase two of his plan: His escape.

He popped the driver's side door, checked one last time that he was on target, and jumped. He landed badly, rolling half-a-dozen times, all the while sliding forward. He was still moving too fast and of he didn't get control, he would face the same fate he had threatened Giolito with.

Bones was about to become a part of history.

Only feet away ahead of him, the two-and-a-half ton Mercedes plowed into the beast, taking him off his feet, driving him back over the edge of the pit.

Bones didn't stop to revel in his success. He didn't stop at all. He couldn't.

But as he reached the edge, he spied the safety

rope he had rigged up earlier next to the spot where the ladder had been. He grabbed ahold of it on his first try, but instead of yanking him to a standstill, both he and it continued forward, right over the edge. From the corner of his eye, he saw that the rope had come loose from its anchor. There was also a lone figure standing near the post where it had been tied off.

Giolito?

But then, just as his momentum carried him over the edge, the rope went taut, and he was whipped into the wall. In the same instant, he heard a tremendous crunch of metal as the SUV smashed into the stone below. The shock wave buffeted him like a hot wind.

A glance down at the explosion of blood beneath the mangled vehicle confirmed the king's final fate.

Still dangling over the excavation, Bones allowed himself to breathe easy. Then, the rope strained, and he was pulled back up and over the edge of the site. Jessie was there, as was Santi and Vivianna. The woman gave him an apologetic nod and stepped aside.

Nico's brothers both held the end of the rope in their hands. They had been the ones to pull him to safety. Nico, however, wasn't with them. He was with the mayor, near the post where the rope had been tied off. He had his knee in the mayor's back, and was holding Giolito's right arm behind him.

"What's going on?" Bones asked.

"That," Nico replied, tilting his chin to the ground beside him.

Lying next to the struggling mayor was a pocketknife. Bones turned and saw that the knot he had tied was still intact. It could still be seen attached to the light post. Giolito had tried to kill him. It's why the rope failed to arrest Bones' death-defying escape.

"You bastard," Bones growled. Jessie softly grabbed his arm before Bones could do anything he'd regret. He calmed and grinned when Nico's brothers stepped next to him. One of them was still holding the rope.

Bones didn't understand a word Giolito said while Nico and the others went about tying him up like a potbelly pig, but it was pretty easy to guess from his tone.

Bones nudged the man with his foot. "Hey, watch your language. There are ladies present."

Off in the distance, the sound of police sirens was audible, growing louder by the second. Bones turned to Nico. "Uh, oh," he muttered with a grimace. "This isn't going to be easy to talk around."

Nico smiled, reassuringly. "Do not worry, my friend. We will take care of this."

Bones pointed at the squirming Giolito. "I don't think he's going to just let it go."

Nico knelt beside Giolito, holding his gaze. "That's exactly what he's going to do. The secret of the Laestrygonians must be preserved, even though they are no more. Leonardo understands this. If the truth were to come out, he would bear the greatest responsibility. You don't want that to happen, do you, Leonardo?"

Giolito glowered, but gradually the fire in his eyes dimmed and shook his head tersely.

Nico turned to Bones. "I will set charges and collapse the tunnels. The deaths of the dig team will be attributed to an accidental cave-in. There will be no further investigation. But I think it would be best if you were not here."

Bones laughed. "I wish somebody would have

told me that yesterday." He glanced over at Jessie. "You think Rose would spring for a few more days in Monaco?"

Despite everything that had happened, Jessie manage a wry smile. "Why would you want to go back there? The Grand Prix is over."

"Who cares about that," Bones shot back. "I don't plan on leaving the hotel room. You did say you'd make it worth my while."

Her smile grew. "Yes I did."

The End

ABOUT THE AUTHORS

David Wood is the USA Today bestselling author of the action-adventure series, The Dane Maddock Adventures, and many other works. He also writes fantasy under his David Debord pen name. When not writing, he hosts the Wood on Words podcast. David and his family live in Santa Fe, New Mexico. Visit him online at davidwoodweb.com.

Matthew James is the critically acclaimed author of eight titles, including *Blood & Sand*, *Mayan Darkness*, *Babel Found*, *Elixir of Life*, *Plague*, *Evolve*, *Dead Moon*, and now, *Berserk*. He lives in West Palm Beach, Florida with his family. You can visit him at:
   www.Facebook.com/MatthewJamesAuthor
   www.JamestownBooks.Wordpress.com
   Instagram: MatthewJames_Author
   Twitter: @MJames_Books